10670398

Also by Patricia Robinson:

Something to Hide

A Trick of Light

A Trick of Light

Patricia Robinson

St. Martin's Press New York

A TRICK OF LIGHT. Copyright © 1994 by Patricia Robinson. All rights reserved. Printed in the United States of America. No part of this book may be used or reproduced in any manner whatsoever without written permission except in the case of brief quotations embodied in critical articles or reviews. For information, address St. Martin's Press, 175 Fifth Avenue, New York, N.Y. 10010.

Design by Basha Zapatka

Library of Congress Cataloging-in-Publication Data

Robinson, Patricia, 1923-
    A trick of light / Patricia Robinson.
       p.   cm.
    ISBN 0-312-10564-9
    1. Women theatrical producers and directors—South Carolina—Fiction.   2. Women detectives—South Carolina—Fiction.
3. Amateur theater—South Carolina—Fiction. I. Title.
PS3568.O3135T75   1994
813'.54—dc20   93-42100
                                      CIP

First Edition: March 1994

10 9 8 7 6 5 4 3 2 1

A Trick of Light

One

"Turning down a chance to act for Sean Mappus! New York! Shakespeare!" Roberta, perched on a bathroom stool, shook her head, went on painting her toenails.

Jervey, all but submerged in the old clawfoot tub, flicked a glance at her mother, then closed her eyes. She spoke with patience. "Ma, you know the group's in a bad way. Since Pa died, they've had at least six directors, all disasters. I just agreed to direct this one play."

"She didn't tell you about the part in the soap opera." Emma, twelve years old, sat on the floor of the spacious, antiquated bathroom playing solitaire. "Big bucks. It beats me." She frowned at the cards. "We could be back in the action instead of stuck in this nowhere town."

"That's enough, Emma." Jervey didn't look up. "Besides, I don't consider eight lines of Shakespeare or playing a doomed teenager in 'All My Tomorrows' as glittering prospects."

1

Roberta became parental. "We all have to begin somewhere."

Jervey opened her eyes, regarded her mother. At sixty Roberta could pass for forty onstage, fifty offstage. Her tall figure was passable even in bikini underwear. Her hair, in a stylish shoulder-length cut, was carefully blond. The strong-boned face had altered slightly, taking on a roguish cast. Jervey marveled at her mother. For thirty-five years Roberta had been the uncomplaining wife of a man dedicated to directing a community theater in a small town on the Carolina coast. Her inherited money all went to maintaining their present abode, Harper Parmalee's ancestral home, a sprawling, comfortable edifice rife with Victorian cupolas, turrets, and verandas. At first, she and Hap, married two days after he graduated from the University of Georgia, barely had eked out a living on the income from seven yearly plays, performed by locals. Before long, Hap's extraordinary talents for directing, scene design, costuming, and particularly for teaching prospective actors produced results that drew audiences from all the surrounding towns. Oldport's inhabitants supported the theater with loyal enthusiasm. A surprising number appeared in plays.

Jervey always found her mother unpredictable, but the big surprise had come two years before, when her father died of a sudden heart attack. Both she and her mother had been severely shocked. Roberta had sat silently in her bedroom for several months, totally withdrawn. She'd even started letting her hair go gray. Jervey, frantic with worry, had postponed her own theatrical career, which consisted mainly of reading for parts she seldom got, to hover near her mother. Then one auspicious day Roberta came downstairs, a striking blonde in a red suit, demanded that Jervey return to New York, and announced that she too was going professional. In record time she had an Actors Equity card, a pretty good agent, and an

2

offer of six months' employment with a regional theater in California. She and Jervey had a rousing farewell party in honor of themselves and closed the house in Oldport.

"What about the Parmalee Players?" Jervey had asked.

For a few seconds she'd seen traces of guilt and sadness in her mother's face, replaced at once by determination. "Hap and I gave the Parmalee Players the best years of our lives," she said. "We laid the groundwork. It's up to them. Sink or swim." Now Roberta, home after a stint of acting with a regional group in Kentucky, claimed she'd returned only to recharge her batteries.

"Why do you keep this big old house?" Emma addressed Jervey. "I mean with you living in New York and Roberta—"

"Mrs. Parmalee," corrected Roberta, eyes narrowed. "We keep it because it's my husband's ancestral home."

"We like to have a place to come back to," Jervey explained. "Besides, there have been Parmalees in this house for eighty years."

"It's damn creepy, if you ask me." Emma shuffled her cards.

Roberta struggled for control. "No one asked you, my dear."

Jervey shot a glance at her mother. "Look, Emma, you've been dying to explore the attic. Why don't you go up there and see what you can find."

"Just don't make a mess," Roberta added, then relented immediately. "There's a big trunk at the far end with a lot of old costumes."

Fully aware that they'd had enough of her, Emma gathered her cards and rose, a plump figure in too-tight shorts and an oversize T-shirt. She shook back a tangle of frizzy red hair, observed them with large brown eyes behind thick glasses,

3

looked around the bathroom, smiled, and gave herself a smooth "drop dead" exit.

Roberta stared at the empty doorway. "Jervey, I swore I wouldn't bring it up again—"

"Then don't."

"I just can't understand anyone leaving their child with a friend so they can shack up with a new lover."

"It's temporary. Deirdre just wants to find out if it's going to work before she springs Emma on him."

"You condone this Deirdre's behavior?"

"I don't condone or condemn. Ma, good or bad, she's my friend. She has problems. I couldn't refuse."

"But to expect you to take on the care of a twelve-year-old child—and a little horror at that." Roberta checked her toenails, screwed the top on the polish. "She's an impossible child. No manners, criticizes everything, this house, the town, the meals, you, me. She's—"

"She's a brat. I know it. But maybe, just maybe she deserves a break, a time when she's not in the middle of one of Deirdre's disastrous relationships, when she's not trying to shut out screams of rage, drunken scenes with two people accusing, forgiving, avenging. She's been palmed off on one friend after another." Jervey stared down at the water, furious to find tears in her eyes.

"Okay, okay."

"Maybe I remember what it was like to be twelve years old and lonely as hell."

Roberta started to the door, stopped. "My! Do I detect an accusation?" She paused. "After all these years you're going to tell me you had a miserable childhood?"

"I didn't say it was miserable."

"Don't tell me you were anything like Emma. You were never a neglected child. We included you in everything!

4

Good Lord, we even had you onstage with us when you were a baby!"

"Exactly!" Jervey shook her head. "Oh, what the hell, let it go, Ma."

"No." Roberta leaned in the doorway. "What precisely did you want that you didn't get?"

There was silence in the large, ancestral bathroom. Jervey squeezed the water from the washcloth, wiped her face. "I guess I wanted to be like my friends, eat meals on time, watch TV together at night, go for Sunday drives." She threw the washcloth back in the water. "Maybe I was stupid, but I wished Pa was a lawyer or a storekeeper or a plumber. I wished we were anything but a damn theater family with weird people always in and out of here, some of them staying for weeks, one opening night after another with all those crises, actors dropping out, actors getting sick, ticket mixups, and you and Pa so caught up in it you didn't see me or hear me—"

"That's not fair!"

The scream from above was loud and shrill. Both women started and looked upward, openmouthed. They stared at each other. They looked upward again. The scream came once more, louder, shriller. Jervey was out of the tub in a flash, grabbing her robe, colliding with her mother in the doorway. Racing ahead, she tore to the end of the hall, up the narrow stairway to the attic, Roberta stumbling after her.

In the poor, late-afternoon light, from two small windows at north and south, they saw Emma crouched behind a large trunk. To one side lay a shambles of old clothes, books. On the floor in front of her gaped an oversize simulated mummy case. What looked like human bones were scattered about, a bare skull lying on its side.

"I'll be damned," said Roberta. Then she laughed.

Jervey stared at the bones. She shivered, felt a sudden,

5

childish terror, and then it was gone. Ashamed at herself, she assumed a tolerant amusement. She picked her way through the debris, feeling the dust cling to her wet feet. "Emma," she said soothingly, "it's okay. It's nothing to be scared of. You upset an old prop, that's all." Emma responded with a gasp followed by a muffled sob.

"It's just something we used in a show," Jervey reassured. "You're likely to find all kinds of things up here. Nothing to fear." She pulled Emma to her feet. "My father made that mummy case for a play. It's made of plywood." She turned over one side with her foot. "Look, you can see where he painted an Egyptian-type face."

"I don't remember a skeleton in *The Man Who Came to Dinner*," mused Roberta. "Someone must have stuck it there as a joke."

Jervey led Emma back across the attic. Roberta surveyed the mess, shrugged. "I keep promising myself to clean up this junk, have a yard sale. That mummy case should have been taken back to the theater years ago. That skeleton, I know exactly where it should be, where it's always hung, just inside the door of the prop room."

After a glass of lemonade and six chocolate-chip cookies, Emma regained her composure. She offered only one comment: "Like I said, this is a really creepy house." Fortified with more lemonade and cookies, she went off to the library, settled into the worn leather sofa, and proceeded to watch *The Sound of Music* for the fourth time.

Jervey needed some privacy, a few quiet hours before that evening's rehearsal. She went to the guest room since Emma had been given the "little princess room," Jervey's tenth birthday present. The privacy was not to be. Roberta, clad in a gold and black kimono, sauntered in and stretched out on the four-poster. She surveyed the room with its flowered wallpaper and matching curtains, the Victorian bureau, chairs, chaise lounge. Lazily she watched Jervey put on underwear, jeans, and a pink shirt. "Amazing," she said. "You still have the figure of a teenager."

"That's why I'm offered all those teenie parts on TV. That's why Sean Mappus would probably cast me as a page. Or if I'm lucky, a Shakespearean boy playing a girl's part."

"Are you implying that you're limited?"

"I'm not implying, I'm declaring." Jervey brushed her short, dark curls without consulting a mirror.

"Jervey, why did you really agree to come back here? Was it pure altruism, concern for the Parmalee Players?"

"I'm not sure."

"Another failed romance?"

"That's it, Ma. He went back to his wife and six children. A divorce would have ruined his chances of being governor."

Jervey threw down the brush, moved across the room, and sat on the window seat. The tangled garden looked hopelessly romantic in the fading light. "I'm just not sure." She turned to Roberta. "Ma, I'm not sure of anything. Sometimes I think I'm a fool, staying on in New York, trying like hell to be an actress. I'm not even sure I can be an actress. I'm programmed for it, that's for certain. There's never been a thought for anything but theater in this house. It was expected of me."

"Hap and I would have agreed to anything you wanted to do. We never pushed you. We never—"

"Oh, no? The day I graduated from college, Pa gave me a list of contacts in New York, promised he'd finance me until I got a break."

"He thought that's what you wanted!"

"He never asked."

"Now, look, Jervey—"

"Ma, I'm not blaming him. Theater meant so much to him, was so important to him that he—"

7

"Frankly," Roberta broke in, "I was surprised. I always thought he'd want you to take over the Players, carry on the tradition." She smiled suddenly. "Maybe he intended you to go to New York, hate the rat race, scamper back home, and become a director."

"Which I seem to have done. At least for a few weeks."

The three of them had supper in the kitchen, sitting at the big round table. Roberta had made a chicken salad and, possibly to impress Emma, a pecan pie. Emma had two pieces. Jervey, worried that Emma still was in mild shock, tried to interest her in the saga of the Parmalee Players.

"It was started by my great-grandfather, Endicott Parmalee, the original Pa Parmalee, back in nineteen-nineteen. He and his wife had a theater company that toured the whole Southeast."

"My husband's grandfather, Endicott Parmalee," said Roberta, "was the youngest son of a prestigious Philadelphia banking family. It just happened that his interests didn't lie in the world of finance."

Jervey went on. "Anyway, they had a son, Orlando, and when he was old enough, he performed along with them. They filled in with the locals in each town. As a matter of fact, Orlando married a local from Savannah, a girl called Stacey Barlow. In nineteen-thirty the Players went broke. Orlando and Stacey were running things by then, the old Ma and Pa Parmalee playing character parts until they died in 'thirty-four and 'thirty-five. It was a bad time. Nobody had money for entertainment. The Players stopped touring. By then Orlando and Stacey had a child, my father, Harper. With a family to support, Orlando got a job."

"Poor man." As if forced, Roberta swallowed a final bite of pie. "After scaling the heights of classical drama, he was reduced to selling men's shirts and underwear at Drehers

8

Department Store. Of course, later he got into real estate. With all that theater background he was a crack salesman."

"What about the Parmalee Players?" Reluctantly, Emma was showing interest.

Jervey smiled. "They survived. Dad's father, Orlando, kept it going, working during the days and directing, building scenery, and training actors at night. His son, my father, went to the University of Georgia on a scholarship. Two months after he graduated, his parents were killed in a boating accident on the Santee River."

Roberta rose, carried her dishes to the sink. "Hap and I were already married. I remember when we heard about the accident. We were at an oyster roast at the Colliers'. We'd been walking on the beach, talking about going to New York and taking a shot at the big time." Roberta stared into the sink. "I knew right then that there'd be no New York, no big time, just a long stretch with the Parmalee Players."

Emma looked hard at Roberta's back. "You sound mad."

Roberta turned to her. "Do I?" She smiled. "Then I misread the line. I would have joined a group of Zulus if that was what Hap wanted."

"True love," muttered Emma.

"Like you say, poppet."

Roberta insisted on doing the dishes. Emma returned to the library and Jervey gathered up her purse and the scripts for the cast and walked out into the twilight to head for the theater. She looked across the wide lawn to the carriage house, built with the same dark brick as the house. Beyond it was a large red barn where various Parmalees had housed livestock in the past and where she'd loved to play as a child. A few years before Hap died, it had been transformed into a dwelling for possible rental. With its glossy wood walls, brick floor, high rafters, and bedroom and bath in the loft, it had a certain rustic charm. The last person to use it had been a senile

9

ex-actor, who'd stayed six months rent free before he was transferred by a reluctant daughter to a rest home in Kentucky.

She had crossed the veranda to the steps when an improbable car, a vintage Bentley, drew up with an air of seasoned elegance and stopped in the driveway. She watched, torn between trepidation and curiosity, as the driver slid from behind the wheel and sauntered toward her. He was the dream of old-time Central Casting, tall, spare, with an aristocratic grace, thick silver hair cresting back from his forehead, not a crease in his pants, safari jacket, paisley ascot. His Gucci loafers shone. His smile beneath a neatly clipped mustache combined optimism and warmth. Jervey knew before he spoke that, in some capacity, he had graced the London stage.

"You must be Jervey." He held out a narrow, manicured hand. "Milo Banford."

She could see him in Shakespeare, in Sheridan, Shaw, Coward. She could see that he carried a worn, expensive suitcase and seemed familiar with his surroundings.

"Dear Milo!" Her mother's voice rose richly behind her. "What a marvelous surprise!"

Before more could be said, Jervey returned his smile and took off. She could hear them going into the house, talking and laughing. Another of Roberta's itinerant friends, undoubtedly "between shows," which meant down on his luck and with no place to roost.

She had too much on her mind to deal with Milo Banford. She would deal only with the Parmalee Players' revival of *The Spelling of Honour.*

She felt a twist of resentment against her mother. Roberta should have mentioned that Milo Banford was coming. Or did she know? Roberta should be more understanding with poor little Emma, see things from other people's points of view. The vehemence behind this litany suddenly was tem-

10

pered by the thought of her mother taking the trouble to assemble most of the original cast of *The Spelling of Honour*. One of the three men had left town ten years ago, after the closing of the play. One of the women was unavailable. It was Roberta who had talked the board of directors of the Parmalee Players into reviving *The Spelling of Honour*. The board, which consisted of a dentist, a postal clerk, a lawyer, a psychiatrist, two teachers, and the head of the local SPCA, had been persuaded earlier by the psychiatrist to do a new play, *Sweet Agony*. He'd extolled its hidden layers of meaning, its exploration of the human condition, and its moments of searing self-confrontation. He'd admitted somewhat modestly that it had been written by his nephew. Yes, Jervey thought grudgingly, she owed Roberta. A part left to be filled was important, but she had a few days to do it. Undoubtedly, Roberta would have a brainstorm.

Jervey loved walking through the town. She didn't start to relive her childhood, but every corner seemed to hold a memory. Pine Street, now neatly paved, once had been at the outer edge of town, almost rural, and called Pine Road then. The Parmalee property had been considered a farm.

She moved farther into town; everything was softened by twilight—the mixture of Victorian and modern houses, the big oaks, pecans, and palmettos. It was an old and rooted community with its own aristocracy. There was a beguiling mixture of naïveté and sophistication, an insistence on a code of behavior that stressed respect for the past and consideration of others. But things were changing. People with different attitudes and values had moved there from other parts of the country. The Accrolux Company had brought in a large affluent group of senior and junior executives, many of whom had bought and restored old houses. There were two very new residential developments, one at the south end of town for blue-collar workers, one at the north end, by the river, for the elite. A shopping mall, just beyond the town, had replaced Drehers Department Store as well as most of the shops on Main Street. Although the old buildings now housed a few shops, many had been converted into small, low-rent apartments.

She walked slowly, remembering the way it used to be. Some of the buildings dated to the late 1800s. A few, like the one with the coy sign OLDPORT OLDE ANTIQUES, were simulated eighteenth-century single houses with small second-story balconies. A drugstore was still in operation, as were two seedy souvenir shops and a modest hardware store.

A call came from the second floor above the Oldport Olde Antiques. A large man loomed between the open French doors, which at one time had led to a wrought-iron balcony.

"Hey, Jervey! Jervey come up an' have a cuppa coffee. Jervey!"

She paused, looked up at him, grinned. "Hi, Sully. Thanks, but I have to get to the theater. You all right?"

"I got doughnuts, Jervey, fresh today. You come up."

"Can't, Sully. Another time. You take care."

She didn't wait to see the disappointment in his face. She made herself move on. The town had changed, but Sully hadn't. Semi-retarded, a simple-hearted, loving man, he'd worked as janitor at the Parmalee Playhouse for as long as she could remember. At all hours he would stand in his window and offer coffee to friends and strangers. An occasional actor would accept. Roberta visited him frequently. Her father used to sit in the tiny, neat, barely furnished room and pretend to play checkers with Sully.

She wondered what the future held for Oldport. Before the Pilgrims settled in New England, the Spanish had arrived there. Then came the French, and later, Scottish and English settlers. By the mid-eighteenth century it was a center of shipping for the surrounding plantations with their harvests of indigo, then cotton and rice. But even before the Civil War, it was eclipsed by Charleston and Savannah and became a shadow of its old self, finally serving as a center for small truck farms and a modest fishing industry.

No one could remember exactly when the town had emerged as a resort and retirement place. For a number of years most of the old plantations had belonged to rich Northerners, but it wasn't until the 1960s that the retirees arrived and, like the Accrolux executives, restored and settled in the old houses or built new ones.

Such a growing population should have provided a large theater audience. Other than exhibits by the Art Guild, there was little offered on the cultural scene. But, since her father's death, the Parmalee Players had gone downhill. A well-meaning but inept board of directors had squandered the group's savings, hired a series of disastrous directors, and, with internecine battling, selected seasons of impossible plays.

Jervey walked down a side street to the harbor. At the north end of a waterfront park, with its palmetto trees, flowerbeds, benches, and a large fountain, was the local marina. Expensive powerboats and sailboats were moored with more modest craft. A sprawling one-story-frame yacht club flew its own banner below the state flag.

Jervey moved slowly, exchanging nods with the black and white families who had come to enjoy the early autumn night. Some had brought their supper and sat on the grass. Children played around the fountain. Old people sat on the benches and looked out at the calm expanse of the harbor.

The playhouse was at the south end of the park. Each time Jervey approached it, she was overwhelmed by memories of her father. It was his bailiwick and his pride. How many times Hap had told her about the hurricane that destroyed the old theater on Main Street, how Hap's father, Orlando, had talked the city fathers into selling the eighteenth-century cotton warehouse for five hundred dollars and how, with a crew of fifty volunteers, he'd turned it into a theater. It was a solid building of English brick. Orlando had bargained with a salvage company that agreed to remove part of the second floor, above what was to be the auditorium, in exchange for the long cypress beams that supported it. The attractive, raftered auditorium emerged. In the beginning, the seats were lengths of canvas stretched over wood supports. It was five years before the group could afford to install proper seats.

Jervey unlocked the double doors. She noticed that the theater sign, hanging from its decorative support, needed repainting. Inside, it was ten degrees cooler. The lobby had a musty odor combined with what she always thought of as an indefinable theater smell. She switched on lights. She glanced at the box office window across the lobby and thought of Hap's favorite sight, people lined up for tickets.

The auditorium was dark except for the work light onstage. It was a wide, generous stage with a high proscenium, backstage depth, enough wing space on either side, overhead height to fly backdrops. On either side, steps led from the auditorium to the stage.

Jervey climbed the few steps at stage right and looked around. Tom Crain, the technical director, had set things up for tonight's reading. Onstage was a long unvarnished table and a collection of straight chairs. At right by the switchboard was a smaller table with coffee maker, paper cups, powdered milk, and sugar. She stood still, fighting nostalgia, recalling her debut in that theater. In a Sunday school play, she'd made a hash of her part, but not this time. With a small role in a children's theater production, she'd remembered all six of her lines. The high point had come when she and the other elves had disappeared down a trap door, still visible downstage, crawled under the stage to an opening at the side of the

14

building, run down the alley to the stage door, and amazed the audience by reappearing on the set a few minutes later.

She put the scripts at one end of the big table, looked at them with trepidation. She hadn't directed since college, but the board of directors of the Parmalee Players believed that the gift was inherited, handed down to each generation like a Sheraton breakfront. She'd been a pushover when Elkin Hughes, board president, had choked up on the phone, talked about the great Parmalee tradition and its possible demise. Just as she'd been a pushover when Deirdre had called and begged that she take Emma "just for a few weeks." She realized glumly that she habitually swayed like a willow in the wind. She was a coward to boot.

Thinking of Emma brought to mind the scene in the attic, the frightened child crouching by the gaping mummy case with its scattered bones. Thank God Roberta had remembered the skeleton in the prop room. She wondered what joker in the cast or crew of that long-ago play had stuffed the bones in the mummy case. The thought of the prop room reminded her of the rolltop desk she planned to use on the set of *The Spelling of Honour*. Hoping it was still around, she switched on the lights beyond the backstage area. A short flight of steps led down to another warehouse, of later vintage, bought by Hap with Playhouse profits. It offered enough space to build sets and store them as well as costumes and props.

Jervey made her way through the construction area, passed the neatly stacked flats, the collection of doorways and windows. She moved into the prop room with its sofas, chairs, tables, lamps, many of them from Oldport attics, donated over the years. Many items had been lost two seasons ago when the current director had decided to have a yard sale to raise money. With relief she noticed that the rolltop desk,

15

covered with dust, was in its usual place. She hoped this was a good omen.

She heard the sound of voices onstage and hurried to greet her cast. She stopped cold. Just inside the prop-room door, dangling from a nail, as always, hung the old skeleton.

Two

There was no time for conjectures about old bones. Sitting at the table onstage facing the cast members, she felt a sharp spasm of uncertainty. She could see the skepticism in their faces. They had the look of people trapped into doing something that defied their better judgment.

"We'll follow the usual schedule." She hoped her smile was welcoming. She divided it among the two women and three men. "We'll rehearse Mondays through Fridays from eight to eleven. We'll open on a Friday, play that Saturday and then Thursday through Saturday of the next two weeks. Tonight we'll have a read-through and tomorrow I'll start blocking scenes."

She knew she sounded too cut-and-dried. She should have set a lighter tone, created what Hap would call a playful attitude. She remembered her father's contagious enthusiasm, the spark in his eyes when he talked to actors. "The important thing," she said, handing out the scripts, "is for us all to enjoy this."

17

She was surprised to discover that Thad Egan, sitting opposite her, still caused her shortness of breath. At fourteen she'd been convinced she would love him forever, that he'd ignore the fact that he was twenty years older, defy convention, and carry her off to happier climes. Roberta, reading the signs in her daughter, had gently implied that half the women in Oldport shared her affliction. Thad Egan, tall, well built, just escaped being handsome. His nose was too blunt, his jaw a bit narrow, but these flaws were offset by thick, beautifully cut dark hair, by wideset dark eyes under heavy brows. To Jervey those eyes sent the message that he understood her on the deepest level, affirmed her unconditionally. At fourteen, all arms and legs and insecurity, she needed only to look once into those eyes to find a new vision of herself. She saw it now as she handed Thad his script. "My God," his eyes were saying, "what a fantastic woman you've become." He didn't look like a corporate lawyer. He looked more like a monarch from an old legend.

With effort Jervey moved her glance to the woman next to Thad, his wife, Abby. Roberta had asked Abby to fill in for Elissa Dowell, one of the two original cast members who wasn't available. Roberta swore Abby had turned in a number of good performances in recent seasons. It wasn't the same Abby whom Jervey remembered from years ago. Gone was the lanky, shrinking nonentity. Gone was the tightly permed, drably dressed creature ever hovering in the wings. Abby's brown hair, unpermed, swept to her shoulders with streaks of gold. Careful makeup had created a model's face. What seemed a bona fide bosom rose and fell under a chic white linen dress. More startling, the shyness had vanished. Abby's glance, now enhanced by aquamarine contact lenses, met Jervey's with consummate confidence. Her smile was charming. It was obvious to Jervey that the same affirmation she'd found in Thad's eyes had worked magic on Abby.

Stanley Botkin's smile was warm, if self-effacing. Everything about him seemed apologetic, the watery blueness of his eyes, the dusty look of his thin blond-gray hair, the nervousness of his stubby fingers. Fairly tall, he gave the impression of being short.

When Jervey attended Oldport High School, Stanley was a science teacher. She remembered the lack of discipline in his class, the ways the kids took advantage of him, ridiculed him. She also remembered the way he'd helped her through a course she otherwise might have failed. She was glad he'd left the school to take a job as a chemist with Accrolux. She was pleased he was in the cast. "He'll play any part, anywhere, in any show," Hap once said. "He's not great, but theater is the bread of life to him."

Fred Hooper, sitting next to Stanley, was at least forty but looked thirty. Swarthy, muscular, in tight jeans and sleeveless T-shirt, he lacked only a tattoo on his arm and a cigarette behind his ear. His rather oily dark hair was pulled into a pigtail, tied with a shoestring. He looks, decided Jervey, like an actor who's played Stanley Kowalski in too many productions of *A Streetcar Named Desire*. No one would guess he was an employee in a feed and grain store.

Lotte Krause, at the other end of the table, chose to remain of indeterminate middle-European origin. She'd come to Oldport twenty-odd years before and for a time ran a second-hand bookstore on Main Street. When this folded, she retired to her cottage at the south end of town where she lived with numerous cats, plants, and recipes.

Jervey guessed Lotte was somewhere between forty and forty-five. Tall and full figured, she had long brown hair streaked with gray and wound around her rather exotic face in thick braids. A past rich in mystery and drama was suggested by her deep, accented voice. Her clothes were ethnic: long full skirts and draped shawls in colorful fabrics.

19

Lotte was an invaluable asset to the theater group. She could play a dowager Russian empress or a starving peasant. With discreet script alterations, explaining her accent, she could play an even wider range of roles.

Jervey plunged in. "*The Spelling of Honour,* as you all know, was a big hit here ten years ago. Despite the fact that it never made it to Broadway, it's still being done by theaters all over the country. I think it's timeless because it deals with unchanging emotions and conflicts within a family.

"You've all played these parts before, except for Abby. Thad, you know that Markham, the father, is divided between honor and greed. Stanley, you know that Dan, as Markham's best friend, is a sycophant who becomes a traitor. Lotte, you're certainly aware that Alma, as Markham's wife, is trying to rediscover the man she married and save him from becoming someone lost and alien. Fred, you can afford to play Avery, the son, as a little older, with time running out, still torn between wanting to see the great man fall and yet needing his love and approval.

"We haven't cast the part of Tim, the younger son, but we will have a Tim by tomorrow night."

Jervey looked around the table. She hoped to find nods of agreement, a flicker of confidence. What she read in their faces was, at best, patience, a resolve to give Hap's kid a chance.

"I appreciate your coming on a Saturday night because of the short rehearsal schedule. Tonight we'll read straight through the play. You don't have to give a performance," she said, echoing Hap's words. "Just make it make sense."

Two hours later they each offered to drive her home, but she declined. She was looking forward to walking at night where one still could walk without fear.

Thad was the last to leave, waiting until she'd switched off the lights. Abby had gone ahead to get a book from her car and give it to Lotte. After she'd locked the big double doors, Thad took her hand, turned her around, pulled her into his arms. It was, thought Jervey, like sinking into a warm tub. She felt no physical attraction, just a moment of peace, assurance.

"All will be well," he said.

He offered again to drive her home, then as she declined, walked off to Abby, who watched from a gray Mercedes.

Jervey returned home the long way, through the waterfront park, past the fountain, flowerbeds, and benches. It was almost deserted. She saw one old man, shuffling toward the end of the dock at the marina. It was warm, with no breeze, no visible moon, and even the lights along the dock looked dim. If this was New York, she thought, I'd be terrified. For no reason, she recalled the skeleton hanging just inside the prop-room door. She laughed out loud, startling a cat that dozed by the marine supply store. There was no reason in the world why the Parmalee Players with their vast supply of furniture, costumes, curtains, flats, and backdrops shouldn't own two skeletons.

When she reached home, she stood in the front yard and stared at the old homestead. Lights shone in the library and kitchen. Roberta and her friend Milo must still be up and about. The house looked rather majestic with its sweeping verandas, intricate latticework, high dormers. She felt a sudden wish to be ten years old again for a few hours, to play croquet on the lawn, soar on the swing that once hung from a branch of the ancient oak beside her.

She could hear her mother's voice across the years. "Jervey, don't leave your bicycle out front. You know where it belongs."

She went into the house, slamming the door to announce her arrival, avoid the unlikely possibility of surprising them at an inappropriate moment.

They were in the library. Roberta in mauve silk lounging

pajamas lounged on the worn leather sofa. Milo sat in a wing chair by the fireplace which was filled with fresh magnolia leaves. On the narrow table behind the sofa a single lamp burned.

"How did it go?" The concern in Roberta's voice was at odds with her physical languor. She toyed with the mint leaves in her frosted silver goblet.

"It went." Jervey sank into the chair opposite Milo. She wondered why she'd never seen an American sit and hold a glass with the same air as the English.

"We're certain to find someone for the part of the son," Roberta assured her.

"No worry," said Jervey. "Tomorrow I'll go down and cover the waterfront or maybe hang around the Y."

"May I fix you a drink, my dear?" Milo rose fluidly. "We're having—"

"Mint juleps." Roberta's voice had a slight edge, a no-smart-cracks-from-you warning.

"Thank you." Jervey smiled sweetly, "I'll have a scotch and water." She watched him cross the room, pass through the dining room into the kitchen.

For a time neither spoke, then Roberta rose, crossed to the fireplace, and turned to her daughter. "Jervey, there's something I want to explain."

Jervey watched her mother, noticed that the cool Roberta looked a bit apprehensive. "Yes?"

"Two things, actually."

"World-shaking."

"Hardly."

"All right, Ma, calm down." Jervey leaned forward, clasped her hands between her knees, and adopted a vocal resonance suitable for the final act of an O'Neill tragedy. "Milo. I know, Ma. I guessed. I saw it the minute I met him.

22

The resemblance. Oh, God, Mother, why did you never tell me?"

"Jervey—"

"I'm trying to understand. Dad busy all the time, you lonely and neglected, dreaming of New York. Milo appears, warm, adoring, irresistible. It was a moment of madness—"

"Dammit, Jervey!"

"I accept it, have no choice. We're all victims, after all. I can't denounce you. We must learn to live with it. Just one thing, though. A small thing."

Roberta's eyes glittered. "Yes?"

"Just don't ask me to call him 'Daddy.' "

Roberta giggled. "He'll be staying in the barn apartment for a while."

"Who is he?"

"An old friend. We acted together at the Goodman, in Louisville and at the Arena in Washington. He's just stopping here to draw a breath."

Stopping to draw a breath, thought Jervey, means no job, no money, no place to stay.

"Emma took to him at once," Roberta added. "Insisted on leading him to the attic to see the skeleton. Later she went to bed like a lamb."

Jervey observed the large, framed poster over the mantel, Pa Parmalee in a 1928 production of *Richelieu*. "Oh."

"Which brings me to the second thing." Roberta picked up something from the coffee table, held it out to Jervey.

"What is it?" Jervey inspected the small, flesh-colored object.

"A hearing aid. It was lying among the bones. Milo spotted it."

"So?"

"It just seems very odd. As I told Milo, the bones are from the theater. They've been there for ages."

"They're not, Ma. The bones you're thinking of are in the old place in the prop room."

Roberta opened her mouth, closed it. At last she spoke. "I think I knew it. Those bones at the theater are wired together. The ones in the attic are loose."

Jervey put the hearing aid back on the table. "Maybe this thing has been lying on the attic floor for years, has nothing to do with the bones."

"It's a thought." Roberta returned to the sofa, stretching out. "But I don't recall anyone in Hap's or my family wearing a hearing aid, not parents, grandparents—"

"Farther back, Ma?"

"Milo says it's a fairly recent model."

"Made within the last ten years or so." Milo crossed the room, handed Jervey her drink. "I've worn a hearing aid for quite a while. If that one was in the mummy case, it more or less dates those bones." He reclaimed his chair, sat, crossed his legs. "Fascinating. I love puzzles. Maybe you didn't notice but one side of the mummy case has a sizable hole. Rats, no doubt. A convenient opening for insects. Once the insects got inside there would be little left but bones. Roberta, you say it was stored in the barn. Was the barn floored at the time?"

"No. Just bare ground."

Jervey felt a bit nauseated. She tried to control it. "What you're saying is that the mummy case could have held more than just bones. It could have been . . ."

"A body," said Roberta reluctantly. "A body stored in the barn and then in our attic all those years."

"When was the mummy case brought from the theater, Ma? And why?"

"I'm trying to remember." Roberta lay back on the cushions. "We used it in *The Man Who Came to Dinner* and that was in the forties. Hap made it for that play. No, wait—we

24

used it again." She turned to Jervey. "The first time we did *The Spelling of Honour,* ten years ago."

"Ma, how did it get in the attic? Why isn't it in the prop room at the theater?"

"I'm trying to remember."

"Dad never stored props like that in the attic; worn-out costumes, maybe, but not—"

"Don't hassle me. I'm trying to think."

Milo pulled a pipe from his pocket. "Do you mind?" he asked Jervey. She shook her head. "There's probably some simple explanation." He carefully directed tobacco from a leather pouch into the pipe, tamped it expertly. "There's no reason to let this upset you."

Jervey was too tired to be upset. She watched Milo, marveled at the way he lit his pipe, took a puff, leaned back in his chair, and smiled at her with paternal warmth. He has a perfect stage face, she thought, that broad forehead, chiseled features, clear hazel eyes. And the voice, resonant with a good range.

"Jervey, I suppose you grew up loving theater. Roberta tells me you made your debut at five?"

"In a church play. I was an angel in the Christmas pageant. I tripped over my robe, broke one wing, and ran howling from the stage."

"I was twelve," he mused, "played Juliet in a boys' school fiasco. In the middle of the balcony scene my voice changed. About half an octave. The audience roared."

"Where was that?" asked Jervey casually. "Eton?"

"Is it so evident? Can you size me up so easily?"

"I'd say Eton, Oxford, and finally, against your pater's wishes, the Royal Academy."

"You're slightly off. Try a Catholic boy's school in Boston, a scholarship to Lehigh, and six months at Actors Studio."

This really jolted her. "You're American?"

"With a British mother. Before marrying my father, a Rhodes scholar from Brooklyn, she'd acted in English rep."

"The closing night of *The Spelling of Honour*," mused Roberta, staring into space. "The play went well but the cast party never got off the ground. It was too big. We combined it with our usual end-of-the-season bash."

Neither Jervey nor Milo seemed to hear her. "But your accent," said Jervey. "Everything about you—"

"Mother coached me." Milo took a sip of his julep. "Remember, this was over forty years ago. Once I showed an interest in theater, she really pitched in. She knew that both onstage and in films, in this country, there were few actors who were believable as what you might term gentlemen. I am her product."

"Was she right?"

"At the time. I was negotiable if not star material, did second leads in New York, pretty good parts in films, and later, much later, a number of forgettable moments on TV. I found it rather difficult to make the transition from gent to cab driver or cop on the beat."

"Wait!" Roberta swung her feet to the floor, sat forward. She stared first at Jervey, then at Milo. "That damn mummy case! It's coming back." She had their attention. "When the play was over, we all pitched in and struck the set. Hap and I left the theater first because we were having the party." Her voice slowed. "We came back here. I saw to the food and Hap set up the kegs of beer. As I said, we expected a big crowd."

"The mummy case, Ma?"

"I'm getting there. Let's see, Hap was getting the beer ready and Sully was helping him."

"The mummy case, Ma?"

"I'm trying, Jervey! The masses had arrived for the party and Hap and Sully and I were in the kitchen. Hap suddenly

26

remembered that the theater group in Beaufort planned to do the same play and asked to borrow some props, including the mummy case. They'd left their truck or van in the parking lot and asked that the props be loaded that night and . . ."

"What, Ma? Think!"

"Someone was to drive it to Beaufort early the next day. Yes! And Hap asked Sully to stop back at the theater on his way home and load the stuff in the Beaufort van." She laughed suddenly. "Of course, he didn't wait. True to form, painfully diligent, Sully left, at the height of the party, went back to the theater, and did as he was told."

"Was the truck driven to Beaufort as scheduled?" asked Milo.

"What? No. After all that, we got a call from Beaufort the next morning, early. They had cast problems, decided to do a revival of *Ladies in Retirement.*"

Jervey took a gulp of her scotch. "That still doesn't explain how the mummy case ended up in our attic."

"Because of the fire! That same night."

"What fire? Oh, I remember. It happened when I was visiting Sage Chalfont up in Charleston," said Jervey.

Roberta explained to Milo, "It was in the prop and storage room that night. God knows how it started. Fortunately it didn't damage the auditorium. Sully, who seldom sleeps, had come back about three in the morning to make sure he'd locked the stage door. He smelled the smoke and called us. We called the fire department. We leapt in our clothes, raced back down there. Lord, what a mess! Not so much what the fire had done but the hoses, water everywhere!"

"And the mummy case, Ma?"

"As I said, the Beaufort group called the next morning, saying they didn't need the props. Since the prop room and storage rooms were awash, Hap had Sully put the props in the theater truck and bring everything back here. We planned to leave the stuff in the barn until the theater dried out."

Jervey picked up the murky sequence. "And the case stayed there until you did over the barn two years ago. It was in the barn for eight years, then put in the attic."

"We should have had it returned to the theater earlier," Roberta admitted. "We just never got around to it."

"One thing bothers me," said Milo. "Supposing there was a body in that case, it must have weighed quite a bit. Wouldn't whoever moved it have noticed this?"

Roberta sighed. "My husband had a bad back. All the moving was done by Sully, who is a general handyman at the theater."

"But even he—"

"Sully is semi-retarded. He enjoys doing what he's told. He's strong as an ox and he questions nothing."

The scream from above made them all jump. Roberta dropped her goblet.

"Emma!" Jervey was on her feet. "I'll go."

"That child is a chronic screamer." Roberta's voice was shaky. She leaned over and tried to brush ice from rug to goblet. "I hope to heaven it's not more bones."

Jervey took the stairs two at a time. She found Emma huddled in the little princess bed with the lamp lit and covers tossed. Framed by the mass of red hair, the small face looked very pale.

"A bad dream, Emma?" Jervey sat on the bed beside her.

"I guess so." She swallowed, blinked. "Do you believe in vampires, Jervey?"

"No, I don't. Vampires are story-telling."

Emma straightened her shoulders, smoothed the sheet with a pudgy hand. "Of course they are. That's what I told my friend Kimberley. It's all made-up stuff." Her face brightened. "Did you meet Milo?"

28

"Yes."

"I like him. He's a real neato guy." She shivered suddenly, looked at the window where the wind tapped the glass with a twig. She shivered again.

"Listen, Emma, how about sleeping with me tonight? I've had a rough day, what with the bones and then the read-through of the play with an incomplete cast. It would be nice to have someone beside me."

Emma was out of bed in a flash. "Sure." She recovered her nonchalance. "A tough rehearsal, huh? That's show biz." She followed Jervey from the room. "If you have bad dreams, Jervey, wake me."

Three

· · · · · ·

When Jervey awoke, Emma was no longer beside her. She could smell coffee as she pulled on her old orange cotton robe, ran her fingers through the short tangle of curls, and padded barefoot downstairs to the kitchen.

The spacious room, the only one in the house with contemporary appliances, including a microwave oven, was flooded with golden light from the double windows over the sink. Copper pots and pans glowed on their hooks above the impressive stove. Sitting at the big round table, Roberta, Emma, and Milo looked up to greet her.

"Milo made eggs Benedict," Roberta announced.

"I'm having doughnuts," said Emma.

Milo rose. "May I fix you a plate, my dear?"

"No, thank you." Jervey moved to the coffee maker on the counter below pine cupboards, found a mug.

"We've been discussing whether or not to call the police," Roberta informed her.

"Roberta, my dear—" Milo looked at Jervey, raised his eyebrows.

"Why, Mother?"

"The hearing aid, Jervey!"

Jervey poured her coffee, looked at them sleepily, aware that she was expected to cast some kind of vote. "Ma, news of that hearing aid is not going to bring Sheriff Sparkman over here with sirens screaming."

Milo looked relieved. "Exactly."

Roberta lifted her chin. "There must have been a body in that mummy case."

"I'm with Roberta." Emma, having conquered her night fears, glowed with excitement.

Jervey knew her mother, the hardheadedness once she'd made up her mind. She could not be deterred, but just possibly, she might be sidetracked. She joined them at the table. "We've got to find more evidence."

"Evidence! Yes!" Emma leaned forward, eyes wide.

"For instance," Jervey groped, "we know that mummy case was last used when we did *The Spelling of Honour* ten years ago."

"Then locked in the barn," Milo helped her, "then stored in the attic."

Roberta was caught up. "That means the body was someone who was at the theater that night."

Jervey sighed with relief. She noticed for the first time that her mother was wearing a faded lavender negligee with a marabou trim from *The Rose Tattoo*. Milo was fully dressed in a beautifully tailored gray suit. Emma was still in her oversize T-shirt nightgown. "Ma, why don't you go through Dad's files, find the program and newsletter for that production. It's a beginning."

Milo sneezed, plucked a marabou feather from his mustache. "A splendid idea."

31

Roberta pushed back her chair. A few more feathers flew. "We'll start as soon as we get back."

"Get back?" Jervey suppressed a yawn. "Get back from where?"

"Church."

"Ma, we've never been regular churchgoers. Weddings, maybe funerals, Christmas—"

"We are when we can't cast a part. Whenever your father was short an actor, he went to one of two places."

"Why don't we go to the other one?" offered Emma.

"The Blue Dolphin Bar isn't open on Sunday."

St. George Episcopal Church had been designed in 1806 for people with modest tastes. Later, a cupola and spire had been added. In the 1840s memorial stained-glass windows proclaimed the affluence of the parishioners. The church was built to accommodate four hundred people. About three hundred now appeared regularly. Built near the edge of town, St. George's stood on a street of old and nicely restored houses, much like the Parmalee homestead. Behind it was a good-sized cemetery with grave markers dating from the year of its inception. Beyond the cemetery stretched an open field and a stand of loblolly pine.

Jervey wore a plain but well-cut dark linen dress with a white collar. Emma, in a too-tight red skirt and off-the-shoulder blouse, stumped like a plump little hen in multicolored wedgies. Roberta, casting herself as a pious churchgoer, wore what she termed a "change of life" print, low heels, and a vintage straw hat. She looked like the spinster secretary of the Ladies' Auxiliary, circa 1940.

They made an entrance. All heads turned, then turned further, not to stare at the females but to get a better look at the marvelous Milo. One can almost feel the melange of conjectures, thought Jervey, as they filed into a pew.

On one side of the altar sat Jake Barnham, a semi-retired

minister who filled in at parishes when rectors were on vacation or tied up elsewhere. He was a big man with lots of white hair, a rosy, seraphic face, and arms that liked to hug. He was much beloved.

On one side of Father Jake was a skinny acolyte who kept twisting his feet to better admire his new Nikes. On the other side sat a young man dressed like Father Jake in cassock and surplice but looking like a refugee from a rodeo, a mountain-climbing expedition, or a safari. Next to him sat Louise Percy, a faded blonde, a perennial lay reader, and a reasonably good actress. She'd played the lead in *The Rainmaker.*

Jervey heard Father Jake greet newcomers and explain that the choir was in Greenville as part of an interfaith concert. She heard the opening prayers and joined in the hymn singing. As discreetly as possible she cased the congregation. The faces were mostly familiar, with a scattering of what she perceived as spiffy senior and junior executives from the Accrolux Company. Their wives looked extremely chic next to the locals. She saw Abby and Thad and, in a pew behind them, Stanley.

". . . and confess our manifold sins and wickedness," prayed Father Jake with fervor. "We should not dissemble nor cloak them before the face of Almighty God our heavenly Father." He never intoned. Each time he addressed God, it sounded not only heartfelt but ad lib.

Jervey's mind kept wandering. She crossed her legs, uncrossed them. Why am I here? she asked herself. Why am I in Oldport instead of New York? Why am I directing a play when I'm not a director? Why have I taken responsibility for a twelve-year-old child and why did she have to find those damn bones in the attic?

She tried to concentrate on the service. Louise Percy, shame on her, was not pronouncing consonants. She dropped the ends of sentences. Two failings that really irked Hap.

". . . all know the young man who will speak to us this morning," Father Jake was saying. "He's spoken here before and I don't have to tell you he has an important message."

Roberta reached across Emma and pinched Jervey's arm, jerked her head to the right. Jervey gave her a glance of exasperation, then saw at once what her mother had spotted. Directly across the aisle was a thin young man, blond, rather frail. The very articulation of his body, the way he sat, held the prayer book, suggested humility, gentleness, an air of isolation.

As if aware of their scrutiny, he turned and, to Jervey's embarrassment, smiled. He was Tim incarnate, the golden, tormented son of *The Spelling of Honour*.

Jervey, filled with sudden hope, took a deep breath, settled back in the pew, and fixed her attention on the lectern.

The speaker was taller even than Father Jake, with darkly tanned skin and sun-streaked hair. From the rugged face came a steady blue gaze. He towered above the lectern.

"I want to read you something from Joseph Campbell's book *The Power of Myth*. He quotes a letter written by an Indian chief to the U.S. Government when it wanted to take over or buy some tribal lands."

Looking at the speaker, she had a sudden moment of complete inner stillness. It was followed by an odd kind of elation, something close to recognition.

"How can you buy or sell the sky?" The deep voice carried the trace of a Low Country accent. "The land? If we do not own the freshness of the air and the sparkle of the water, how can you buy them?"

Jervey half heard the words, but they were mixed with her father's words. "Don't worry about your inner feelings, the hidden motivations of your character; play the scene. Play on each other; prompt reactions."

"We are part of the earth and it is part of us. The perfumed

34

flowers are our sisters. The bear, the deer, the great eagle, these are our brothers."

There was a cadence to the words that lulled her. She was reminded of her one real love affair, a painful disaster. Jason used to read his poems to gatherings in friends' lofts on Sunday afternoons. Sometimes Lowell Granger backed him up on the flute. She recalled that certain people, those more gainfully employed in theater, music, or publishing, sat on sofas or chairs. She recalled the hardness of the floor against what Jason referred to as her "skinny little butt."

". . . remember that the air is precious to us, that the air shares its spirit with all the life it supports . . . so if we sell you our land, you must keep it apart and sacred, as a place where man can go to taste the wind . . ."

Her friend Laura had called Jason "a hello-goodbye man." She thought of her final scene with him. "You're going as a new woman, a free woman, Jerve, but it's surface, a case of the trendies. Actually, visions of sugarplums dance in your eyes, sugarplums and the Christmas tree and the kiddies lined up with their stockings and a sign over the door that says 'Forever.'"

"The earth does not belong to man, man belongs to the earth. Man did not weave the web of life, he is merely a strand in it."

Jervey, half listening, reviewed Hap's theory about relationships on- and offstage. He'd found part of it in a Karen Horney book, part he'd added. "In regard to each other," he'd claimed, "you are moving toward, away, against, above or with. Each scene boils down to this. The dramatic punch depends upon how these attitudes change within the scene."

"What will happen when the secret corners of the forest are heavy with the scent of many men and the view of the ripe hills is blotted by talking wires? Where will the eagle be? Gone!"

She had not been aware of listening. Her mind had been too crammed with her own concerns. Was it her subconscious mind that heard him, was touched, sent a tear sliding down her cheek? She looked hard at him. The big, muscular body was not designed for cassock and surplice, the hands clutching the sides of the lectern were long, but a workman's hands.

"Hold in your mind the memory of the land as it is when you receive it. Preserve the land for all children and love it, as God loves us all."

At the end of the service Roberta was out of the church like a shot, barely nodding to people she knew, sidestepping the mob lined up to shake hands with Father Jake. Milo, Jervey, and Emma scampered after her. Jervey had no chance to speak to her mother until they'd reached Milo's Bentley, parked halfway down the street under a pecan tree.

"Ma, slow down! We've got to find out the name of that man across the aisle."

They all climbed into the car. Roberta pulled off her dismal hat. "I just saw Billy Strang. He played opposite me in *The Four-Poster*. And now meeting me in this getup! Lord, I had no idea he was back in town."

"Ma, the man across the aisle, we've got to know who he is. He's perfect for the part."

"Billy was really quite mad about me. Hap was amused."

"That man, we've got to arrange a meeting, Ma. Today!"

"Billy always said I reminded him of Julie Christie."

"Julie who?" asked Emma.

"Julia Roberts," snapped Roberta.

Between the church and Main Street they argued heatedly about whether or not to go home and cook a big Sunday dinner. They ended up at Clem's Chowder Cafe, where they were served the day's special, fried chicken, crab cakes, hush puppies, red rice, cowpeas, fried okra, cole slaw, and deep-

36

dish blueberry pie. From their table by the window they could see much of the little harbor with its sailboats, power-boats, shrimp trawlers, and circling gulls. Jervey picked at her food, still annoyed with her mother. Roberta chewed absently, staring at her plate. Milo regarded the food with some astonishment, but ate politely. Emma ate only her chicken, remarking that she had a friend who lunched every Sunday at the Plaza.

They went back to the house, changed into more comfortable clothes, and settled in the library. All but Roberta, who disappeared. Milo read the Sunday *New York Times,* Jervey toyed with the crossword puzzle, and Emma played solitaire. When Roberta finally appeared, she still wore the "change of life" print and carried some notepaper.

"I made some phone calls," she reported.

All heads lifted.

"Father Jake and Anna Louise Dobbs—"

"The man across the aisle, Ma?" Jervey was on her feet. "You've got his name?"

"More than that. Lord, Anna Louise knows everything about everybody. His name is Arnold—"

"Schwarzenegger!" cried Emma.

"Arnold Brian."

"Arnold Brian." Jervey vocally savored each syllable. "It even sounds theatrical."

"Son of a vice-president at Accrolux. Went to Choate and Yale. And—are you ready for this—majored in fine arts and went on to get his M.A. in drama!"

Jervey fell back on the sofa, weak with relief. "Oh, Ma, it's too good to be true! Oh Lord, how marvelous! Can Anna Louise get us an introduction? Look, she could have us over for a drink and invite him, too? I mean, I can't just call him up and ask if he wants to be in a play. I can't grab him on the street and say, "Arnold Brian, I need you. I can't—"

37

"There's a drawback," said Roberta evenly.

"A drawback?" Milo put down the newspaper.

"He's already signed up for a season on 'All My Children,' " said Emma, shuffling her cards.

"He has problems." Roberta spoke with reluctance.

"He's wanted by the F.B.I.," said Emma.

Roberta frowned, turned to Jervey. "He's an addict."

"Drugs?" Milo shook his head.

"Since prep school. He's been in some clinic upstate. Comes home for weekends now and then."

"No!" Jervey stood up.

"It's not hopeless!" Roberta's eyes sparkled. "Being in a play could be the best possible thing for Arnold. He loves theater, has had training—Yale Drama School is excellent—I mean this would give him some motivation, a reason to lay off the drugs. Lord, it could be this poor young man's redemption, save him from—"

"No, Ma! And I mean, no!" Jervey ran from the room, streaked up the stairs.

Four

She sat in her sunlit room and finally succeeded in overcoming her disappointment. At one point she was able to laugh about it. She began to go over her script, her father's copy of the play, complete with blocking directions, light and sound cues. In the back, shorthand comments on the actors in that production were drawn in Hap's special hieroglyphics which were incomprehensible to Jervey. She held the script with a certain reverence, as if holding a part of her father's life.

Her exasperation with Roberta faded. She was remembering Hap's optimism. He wouldn't be found moping about because he was short one actor. He'd know that either he'd find someone or someone would show up. In all the years he'd directed, he'd never abandoned a play or canceled a performance. Hap, because he loved theater with such passion, believed in miracles.

In her underwear she stretched out on the bed, stared at the ceiling, and thought about Emma. Emma should be leading a normal life, a child's life, going to school, to friends' houses, to birthday parties. It was fall and she should be entering the sixth or seventh grade.

"Don't worry about that," Emma's mother, Deirdre, had told her. "The child has an off-the-charts IQ. So she misses a semester, so what?"

Deirdre was more a child than Emma, invariably putting herself first, forever changing lovers, jobs, apartments, lifestyles in quest of an identity that should have included the fact that she was a mother. Jervey was sure that it never dawned on Deirdre that smartass Emma was a confused and deprived little person with a very uncertain future. And what on earth can I do about it? she asked herself, instantly withdrawing the question.

As she drifted toward sleep she thought hazily of the bones in the mummy case, the hearing aid. Props, she assured herself, with some amusement, for a TV mystery, concocted by the four of them. Nearer sleep came a non sequitur, words she'd heard in church that morning, ". . . a place where man can go to taste the wind . . ."

When she awakened later that afternoon, the sun was making a spectacular exit. She stood by the window watching colors melt together over rooftops, through gardens and, to the north, the tall pines. She put on the old orange cotton robe and once more walked barefoot downstairs. She must check on Emma. After all, the child was her responsibility. Maybe she could play cards with her or bake some cookies. She felt ill equipped to be a surrogate mother.

There was no sound from downstairs. Apparently everyone had gone out. She was in the library before she realized that someone was sitting absolutely still in a wing chair by the fireplace. At first, she didn't recognize him without the cassock and surplice. He wore khaki pants and a dark blue blazer. His tie was a bit loosened.

He rose. Like two six-year-old strangers they simply stared

40

at each other. Jervey briefly considered excusing herself and running upstairs to put on clothes. She moved to the sofa as if clad in a smart black sheath and high-heeled Ferragamo sandals, motioned to him to sit, and sank down herself with marvelous grace.

She was about to stun him by saying, "Tell me about yourself," when he spoke. "Your mother is fixing me a drink."

Suddenly it dawned on her. Roberta had not been idle that day, her mind going at top speed. How many flimsy alternatives had her mother discarded? How many phone calls had she made? Jervey faced what she was sure was her mother's bottom-of-the-barrel solution to the part of Tim. She groaned inwardly. Was Roberta so desperate she'd forgotten that the character of Tim was described as thin, pale, tormented, ever in flight? What sat before her was a muscular, darkly tanned, and singularly untormented specimen, who obviously never was frightened into anything resembling flight.

She crossed her legs and they both stared at her bare feet. She pulled up her legs, tucked her feet under a cushion. "I'm Jervey," she said.

"I know."

Another pause.

She seldom was tongue-tied, but those two lines of dialogue offered no sparkling possibilities.

They sat in silence. He didn't seem ill at ease, but was inspecting her with great care. She considered babbling. Once Jason had called her a typical southern female babbler. The occasion was a Sunday poetry reading, a lengthy rendering of Jason's latest effort in front of an audience of his peers. At the end of it, no one spoke. They were still as stones. Trained by Roberta to establish social ease and keep things moving, she'd been the first to speak. And the second, and the

41

third, resulting in a monologue that neither charmed nor elicited further conversation. Later, when she'd commented to Jason on the odd lack of interchange, he'd looked at her with a clever mixture of saintly patience and monumental scorn. "We speak," he said, "when we have something of meaning to say."

"I'm Chance Crown."

"I beg your pardon?"

"Chance Crown, my name."

"Oh."

"You have trouble with that?"

"No. Of course I don't. But it's unusual. Kind of Shakespearean. 'By what dark fortune wear I this chance crown'?"

"Is that a direct quote?"

"I made it up. He wouldn't mind."

"Actually, it's Magnus Chance Crown."

"I can see why you opted for Chance. My name is Titania Jervey Parmalee."

"I saw you in church this morning," he commented.

"Reverend Chance Crown; it has a nice ring," she said. "Your sermon was very impressive." She thought of the tear sliding down her cheek. "Very moving."

"Thank you. I didn't think you'd heard." He smiled. "You were busy giving the congregation the once-over."

"A nervous habit," she said quickly. "Like a tic."

"And I'm not a reverend. I just talk in churches now and then."

"You're not a minister?"

"Nope."

"You were defrocked?" she asked hopefully.

"Not even that."

"Oh." She'd envisioned a dramatic loss of faith, a tormented dark night of the soul.

"You've met!" Roberta swanned into the room wearing

42

her mauve lounging pajamas. "Forgive me for taking so long, Chance." She handed him his drink, casting a brief, censoring glance at Jervey's orange robe. "Milo and Emma have gone for a walk, Jervey." She drifted into a chair opposite their guest. "I told Chance that we all were so moved by his talk that he simply had to come for a drink and let us thank him in person. " 'The earth does not belong to man,' " she quoted dreamily, " 'man belongs to the earth.' "

" 'A place where man can go to taste the wind,' " Jervey found herself saying.

He leaned in a little, looked from one to the other. "That letter, that beautiful letter, it explains a big, frightening problem so simply. Somehow we've got to make people aware of what's happening, how much land is being bought, sold, destroyed."

"I couldn't agree more," said Roberta. She paused for a decent interval, then went on. "Tell us about yourself," she spoke gently. "And forgive me for being a nosy old lady. You grew up here?"

"A few miles away. I'm a country boy."

Wonderful, thought Jervey. She could see a deprived childhood, failed crops, scrabbling for food, a father who beat him with an old harness.

"It was a great place to grow up. There were five of us kids. My brothers and I spent days wandering barefoot through the marsh, hunting, fishing, catching snakes." He laughed. "Occasionally blowing up an old outhouse or raiding a watermelon patch." He stopped, obviously sure that he'd been babbling.

"Then what?" asked Roberta avidly.

I don't believe it, thought Jervey, she's still hoping for Juilliard.

"Dad always called us 'the swamp rats.' "

"School?" Roberta pressed smoothly. "Your job now?"

43

"School?" He paused. "Well I didn't settle down until the last year of high school. Then I had two good teachers who really made a difference. I went on to Cornell."

"Cornell!" Roberta was charmed. "I've heard they have a very good drama department."

"I wouldn't know much about that. I was into environmental ecology."

"Of course." Roberta tried not to look deflated.

Jervey observed him with some amazement. His complete openness verged on naïveté. It somehow was at odds with his particular kind of poise. "What did you do after Cornell?"

"Waiter, house painter, stevedore."

"And now?"

"Conservation officer with the State Wildlife and Marine Resources Department."

"Oh," said Roberta and Jervey in unison.

"And you?" he asked, looking at Jervey.

"Me?" She hadn't expected this or his unwavering gaze.

"I know about your family and the theater; everyone does. What else?"

"What else?"

His smile was broad, his teeth very white. "Were you ever a swamp rat?"

"No. No, I can't say that I was."

"She was the baby Jesus in the church nativity when she was only three months old," bragged Roberta.

"And then?"

"Grade school and high school here, later, college, some acting in New York."

"You've been away a lot, haven't spent much time here."

"I guess not."

"It's a great place to be."

"Is it?" She had the feeling he was half teasing her.

"Land of the hardwood swamps, the black-water rivers,

barrier islands, coastal marshes, ancient ricefields, cathedral forests." Their glances locked.

Roberta had had enough of this. She put her glass on the coffee table, flung back her hair, settled against the cushions. "Chance, tell me," she spoke in her silkiest tone, "have you ever been on a stage?"

Jervey didn't speak to her mother until later when they were in the kitchen making shrimp pilau. Milo, wearing an apron, was cutting up tomatoes, Emma dicing celery and peppers, and Roberta peeling shrimp. By the time Jervey had lined up the spices on the counter, she felt controlled enough to address Roberta.

"Tell me again what he said."

"He said he'd give it a try."

"What was his attitude?"

For once, Roberta didn't hedge. "Well, he did look a little stunned, no, not stunned, more surprised at himself. But he said he'd be at the theater tomorrow night. Incidentally, Jervey, it was a bit rude of you to leave the room just before I popped the question."

"I stayed until you casually remarked that our houseguest is a philanthropic millionaire interested in wildlife preservation."

Milo spoke up. "Your mother has great powers of persuasion."

"All the Roberta Parmalee penultimate ploys. Ma, this poor guy isn't interested in theater. He'll wake up tomorrow and wonder what hit him. He'll call and say he has to sit up with a psychotic heron."

"I like his looks," commented Emma. "Real macho."

Jervey glanced at Roberta. "The character in the play is supposed to be scared of his own shadow."

The child persisted. "But isn't that what acting's all about?

Daryl Cates played a wimp in *Tower of Fear* and a hit man in *Cornered*."

"Ma, there's a name for this kind of coercion. It's called—"

"Improvising." Roberta smiled.

The atmosphere was less strained during supper. The shrimp pilau was delicious, the salad outstanding. Milo amused them with stories about theater mishaps. Roberta recalled a night when Milo, sitting downstage in full view of the audience, realized his fly was unzipped. With no consternation and taking his time, he'd risen, turned upstage to a drink table, refilled his glass, zipped his zipper, and returned to position. The audience gave him a hand.

"What about the bones?" Emma interrupted their laughing. "You said we were going to get evidence."

Roberta composed herself. "The child is right. We've been so overcome by the needs of the moment that—"

"Ma, there's some simple explanation for those bones."

"But not," said Milo, observing Emma's eagerness, "for the hearing aid."

Roberta picked up her cue. "I found the newsletter and program for that show. I phoned around. As far as I can see all are alive and accounted for."

Milo took out pipe and tobacco pouch. "All still in town, cast and backstage crew?"

"Yes. It was a small cast and a one-set show. The cast doubled as crew."

"Ushers?" asked Emma.

"Girl Scouts. Every night." Roberta frowned. "Of course Keith Lynch, the man who played Tim, left town after the last performance."

"Keith Lynch." Milo filled his pipe. "Gone." He noticed Emma leaning forward avidly. "You waved him off?"

"Of course not. But he must have gone. There was the usual confusion after the final show, everyone getting ready

46

for the party at our house. It was the end of the season and we'd invited all the actors from all the shows. As I remember, Keith didn't come to the party. I think he wanted to get somewhere special that night."

"He never came back to Oldport?"

"Not that I know of. He was here for just a few months, doing some writing. He'd rented a house out on the Point."

"How did he happen to be in the play?" asked Jervey. "No, don't tell me. You—"

"Your father found him in the Blue Dolphin bar. Hap had an infallible instinct. He could watch someone for an hour or so and know if he was teachable, directable. As it turned out, Keith had acted for a number of community theaters."

Jervey knew that the discussion was for Emma's entertainment. "I trust he looked the part, Ma. Unlike Mr. Chance Crown."

"He was Tim in the flesh. Very slim, graceful, very blond with a face that was both spiritual and a trifle decadent. Women adored him." Her memory stirred, she went on. "And what a dancer! I remember one Saturday night at the club, people clearing the floor for them."

"Them?"

"Keith and Elissa Dowell. Elissa was playing the daughter in *The Spelling of Honour*," she explained to Milo. "My God, they were like Fred and Ginger. They—"

"Incidentally," Jervey broke in, "why isn't Elissa doing her old part?"

Roberta looked at her with surprise. "I thought you knew. The town tragedy. A complete breakdown, alcohol, drugs, the works." She stared at her empty plate. "We all were stunned. I mean, Elissa was the town belle, had everything, gorgeous looks, a rich daddy, lived in that mansion. What's more, she and Thad Egan were the golden couple."

"Now I remember," said Jervey. "I remember that she and

47

Thad were dating and then suddenly they weren't." Most of all, she remembered her own relief, the hope that now Thad would wait for her. Then, some time later she'd heard that he'd married Abby.

"When did this happen?" inquired Milo. "Elissa's breakdown."

Roberta racked her brains. "Let's see, we were doing *Rashomon* when we heard about it, so it must have been about ten years ago."

"The same year Dad did *The Spelling of Honour.*"

"I guess it was."

Nobody said anything. Finally, Milo spoke. "You heard no more from Keith Lynch?"

Roberta sighed. "Not that I remember. He wasn't the cozy type who sends postcards. Besides, none of us knew him that well."

"What does it say in the newsletter, Ma, where it tells about everyone in the cast?"

Roberta went to the library and came back at once with the four-page flier. She handed it to Milo and watched him put on rather flattering horn-rimmed glasses.

"Here it is. 'We welcome Keith Lynch (Tim) making his local debut. Keith describes himself as a bird of passage, an itinerant writer, moving from state to state in his quest for material. What's known as an army brat, he's lived all over the world, is proud of being largely self-educated. In various theaters he's appeared in such plays as *Hay Fever, Richard the Second, Waiting for Godot,* and *Scruples.*' "

"A man from nowhere," said Milo, "with no traceable background, heading for parts unknown. Roberta, is there anything additional about him in the program?"

"No. You know, either he wasn't expected anywhere or he was and then arrived safely. If a missing-person claim had been filed and our police department contacted, they would have questioned everyone at the theater. A drifter," she mused, "going from one town to another, gathering material for a book, appearing in local plays."

"Ma, where was he before he came to Oldport?"

"Oh, Jervey, I don't know. I don't remember. It was years ago and besides he wasn't very communicative."

"Maybe we should talk to that Melissa," suggested Emma.

"Elissa," corrected Roberta. "No hope. From what I hear she's really out in the hollyhocks."

"What about the other people in that play?" persisted Emma.

"The child has something," said Milo.

"No!" Jervey spoke firmly. "I don't want my cast all stirred up over this thing. Directing this play is going to be hard enough without a crazy private murder investigation."

"Besides," Emma spoke through a yawn, "someone in her cast might be the real villain."

At Roberta's urging they all headed for their rooms. When Jervey walked into hers, after taking a shower, she found Emma once more in her bed, sound asleep. She sighed, crawled in beside her, exhausted.

Even though she longed for sleep, her mind refused to call it a day. She hoped it wasn't going to be a night of jumbled thoughts, surrealistic dreams about old bones, about turning Chance Crown into an actor in record time. What an odd person he was, so open, so straightforward, and yet so utterly different. She thought of the look in his eyes when he described his childhood, the Low Country. Her friends in New York would be appalled and amused by his lack of cool. She thought again of the blunt-featured face, the callused hands gripping the lectern, the awed voice reading the Indian's letter. She could hear Jason saying, "Is this joker for real?"

Five

Jervey spent the next day with Emma. They drove to the shopping mall in Roberta's old Toyota and replaced some of the clothes in Emma's deplorable wardrobe. Emma's taste proved surprisingly conservative. After selecting two pairs of well-fitting jeans, some T-shirts, and sneakers, she opted for pleated skirts, one plaid and one a soft blue. Jervey added a pair of black flats for dress.

"If you keep track of what you've spent," ordered Emma with a worried look, "she'll pay you back."

"I know. Don't worry about it." Jervey refused to review what she'd charged on her credit card. What's more, she knew that expecting to be reimbursed by Deirdre was living in a dream.

They didn't go to Clem's Chowder Cafe or the Oldport Inn for lunch. Using tact, laced with some firmness, Emma suggested the Burger King she'd spotted near the mall. After lunch they walked down the main street of town. Emma watched Jervey nodding to some people, stopping to talk to others. Finally she was obliged to comment, "Do you know everybody in this town?"

"It's not very big, Emma. And, remember I grew up here. Of course there are a lot of new people I don't know."

"Weren't you bored, growing up here?"

"No, I wasn't bored. There were lots of things to do. I had basketball, school, choir, plays. There were parties, fairs, track meets. I had friends. Holidays were best, especially Christmas."

"I think Christmas is a real drag."

"I loved it. Ma and Dad and I would go out in the woods and cut a tree and some smilax to wind around stair rails. On Christmas Eve all the theater people would come by. We'd have a big bowl of eggnog for them and the carolers—"

"You're kidding!" Emma managed a look of utter scorn. "It sounds just like 'The Waltons.'"

"I can't see you sitting in front of a TV, watching 'The Waltons.'"

"Old reruns, late at night, when there's nothing else on."

That night, when Jervey, armed with a carefully studied script and what she hoped was fortitude, reached the theater, she found the door unlocked. Inside, Sully lumbered across the lobby with his broom. He stopped, dropped the broom, and gaped at her with pleasure. At six foot four, he had the body of a wrestler and a round, outsize child's face.

"Jervey! I help Tom put out the coffee and cups. We count the cups, him and me." He smoothed his hair, cut short and neatly parted. "An' the chairs by the table."

"Thank you, Sully." She smiled at him, patted his arm. Sully's face seemed capable of only three expressions: delight, confusion, and woe. "The theater looks great, Sully, nice and clean."

"I keep it clean, Jervey. Real clean."

"I know you do." She'd not planned what she said next.

51

"Sully, do you remember the old mummy case we used in the plays *The Man Who Came to Dinner* and the first *The Spelling of Honour?*"

"Mommy case," he echoed blankly.

"Ten years ago, you moved it from the theater to a truck, then into our truck. You and Hap drove to the house and you put the mummy case and some other things in the barn."

"Mommy case, Jervey?"

"Think, Sully."

He wore his look of confusion. He was thinking hard. He shuffled his feet, rubbed his hands together, then stood very still, woebegone.

"It's all right, Sully. Don't worry about it. It's not important. My, this old place looks good, clean as a whistle." She beamed at him and he beamed back. As she started down the aisle, he picked up his broom, still grinning.

When she was a child she often shared her toys with Sully. He loved the little trucks, spinning tops, even the paper dolls. When she was about six, Hap explained to her about Sully, why he was different from other grown-ups. At first she didn't understand, then Hap told her that maybe Sully was like Peter Pan and would be a child forever.

Tom Crain, the technical director, was checking the switchboard. Short, with red hair and beard, he reminded Jervey of an Irish bartender. He'd been hired after Hap's death when Joe Frazier had left to work for a movie company in North Carolina. With the help of volunteers Tom built and painted sets, usually on weekends. He spent his days working at the marina repairing boats.

The set was in place, partially painted and with most of the furniture arranged. He must have hustled, thought Jervey, to get things ready for tonight's rehearsal.

"A lot of those autotransformers have to be replaced with

52

solid-state dimmers," he said without preamble. "And you really need to get a computer-controlled board."

"I'll make a note, Tom." Like so many of the tech people she'd known, he was habitually pessimistic and defensive. Her father once had described it as "egofibrotechnitis," brought on by hostility toward actors, a feeling that "those bastards get all the credit."

"Tom, your set design worked out beautifully," she affirmed him.

"Yeah?" He looked up from the antiquated switchboard.

"The green walls"—she groped to find a compliment—"the symbolism, very clever." He looked at her as if she'd lost her mind. "Green," she pressed on, "the color of envy, that's the theme of the play, envy, greed."

"Yeah. Sure. You need me anymore tonight?"

"No. I'll lock up later."

He headed for the steps leading to the auditorium, then turned. "This your first directing job?"

"Well, yes. I mean, no. Not exactly."

He surveyed her, head to toe. "Lots of luck."

As she watched him leave, she saw another figure moving down the aisle. Chance Crown wore muddy boots, wrinkled work clothes, and a look of anticipation. He scaled the stairs to the stage in two steps, followed her gaze to his boots, and laughed.

"I didn't have time to go home and change."

"Don't worry."

"I came early. Thought you might want to fill me in."

She wondered if he really smelled of fresh air and pine or if she imagined it. "I'll start blocking the play tonight, showing everybody where they move, entrances and exits. It's not complicated."

"If you say so." His smile was relaxed.

Tall herself, she felt small next to him, not because of his

53

size, but his seemingly effortless control of himself and his surroundings. Hadn't it dawned on him that he was going to get up in front of hundreds of people and quite possibly make a fool of himself?

"We'll start with the basics." She explained stage left, right, and center, upstage and downstage. She showed him how to sit in a chair without looking, to rise easily. She explained the stillness needed during another actor's important lines.

His concentration was heartening. She gave him his script and was about to tackle the problem of phrasing when the rest of the cast arrived, moving down the aisle, en masse, with a singular lack of anticipation.

As they climbed to the stage they managed a group smile, Thad's the most convincing. They were casually dressed. Even Lotte had abandoned her gypsy draperies for pants and a man's shirt. Only Abby was well turned out, wearing an inappropriate pale blue silk pants suit.

"Jervey, I'm going to need a lot of help. I've never tried a part this big."

Jervey looked into the earnest eyes behind aquamarine contacts. What she saw was an insecurity that bordered on desperation. She saw the shy, mousey secretary pretending to be Thad Egan's perfect wife. "Abby," she touched her arm, "I'll give you all the help you want. You're going to be fine."

She introduced Chance to the rest of the cast. They inspected him with some amazement and what Jervey perceived as a deepening consternation.

"Well," she chirped cheerfully, "shall we start the blocking? I'm using Hap's directions, so I'm sure a lot of it will be familiar to you."

Things moved more smoothly than she'd dared hope. As she watched the original cast entering, exiting, sitting, standing, once more at home on the set, she felt encouraged. Thad, who'd had to gray his hair for the part ten years ago, looked far more convincing as the father. Stanley's watery blue gaze had not changed, but the added years of being ingratiating to the world had given him an air of hardened sycophancy, like an aging Iago, perfect for the traitorous friend.

Lotte was still Lotte, dusky earth mother with the black braid hanging over one shoulder, rich contralto voice commanding attention. Time had slowed her a little. The dark eyes smoldered less, reflected more.

Fred, stocky, dark as Lotte, with a much shorter pigtail, fitted more than ever the part of the rebel son. The fact that he now looked older would make the character almost pitifully foolish, much more poignant.

Abby presented a problem. The daughter in the play was defined as a woman who, like the son, Tim, habitually faded into the woodwork, neither saw nor made use of her own beauty. In her smart pants suit and with her carefully made-up face, Abby looked like she was ready to lunch with friends at the club and control the conversation. At least, Jervey told herself, Abby had admitted that she needed help.

After all three acts had been blocked, there was a run-through. Chance's concentration was admirable. He was obligingly still during other characters' lines, had an innate sense of good phrasing, didn't drop the ends of his sentences, and enunciated his vowels. Unfortunately, with his height, fine posture, and deep resonant voice, he dominated the stage. Raw as he was, he had genuine stage presence. He was all wrong for the part of Tim. Without some miracle he'd throw the whole play off balance.

They stopped for a coffee break and Lotte produced a large pastry box. On the lid was a design of daisies and violets with the logo "From Lotte's Kitchen." "A friend sent me the boxes," Lotte explained. "Just got them today. A bit coy, maybe, but useful."

The cast, sharing the kuchen, was more relaxed. Thad and

Chance talked about a land trust project. Lotte observed Chance with evident appreciation. Stanley and Abby gossiped about a scandalous occurrence at the yacht club on Saturday night. Fred, slouched in a chair, fingered his pigtail and read a sports magazine.

Jervey stared at her coffee mug, trying to decide what her father would do about Chance. She was stuck with him. She knew Hap would begin with physical articulation, the handling and movement of the body. She looked across the stage at Chance's big, muddy boots, despaired.

After a fifteen-minute break she stood. "Let's go through all the blocking again. This time—"

"Jervey?" Sully's voice echoed in the theater. His face alight, he hurried down the aisle. "Jervey? I remember!" He climbed the steps, grinned at everyone on stage. "The mommy case, Jervey. I remember!"

"Never mind, Sully." She didn't need this, explaining about the bones to these people. "It doesn't matter, Sully."

"But I remember!" He tried to speak with care. "Mommy case was wet. I put mommy case in one truck, then in Hap's truck, then next day in Hap's barn. Hap got bad back, but I'm strong, Jervey. I got strong arms. I carry mommy case up the steps to the—"

"I know, Sully."

"I put in Hap's attic!"

Somehow she got Sully back down the aisle, out of the theater and on his way home, sidestepping any curiosity about his outburst. They had one more run-through and by eleven o'clock Jervey had managed to take them through half the first act for interpretation.

The rehearsal ended. The cast trailed off to their cars. Thad stopped to tell her how well she was doing, that Hap would be proud of her. She watched him hurry down the aisle to Abby, who took his arm as they left. Lotte called from the front of the theater to tell her she'd put the rest of the kuchen in the office and she must take it home to Roberta.

Chance lingered until they'd all gone. "Jervey, don't lose heart. I'll do better." He looked amused.

"You're doing fine." She started up the aisle, stopped. "Look, do you think you might be able to take smaller steps?"

"Smaller steps?"

"And maybe slouch a little?"

His amusement deepened. "I could try."

She didn't know where to go from there. He was standing close to her in the dim theater; everything about him, size, presence, even scent, confused her, unnerved her. She hurried up the aisle.

"Can I give you a ride home?"

"No thanks, Chance. I like to walk." She was having trouble breathing. She decided she was more tired than she thought.

Walking down the silent street she realized that she'd forgotten Lotte's cake. No matter. It would keep until tomorrow night. She strode briskly, taking deep breaths. She dared to congratulate herself on the success of the rehearsal. The cast was going to be good. She felt sure she could help Abby, lead her into an understanding of the part. That left Chance as the only big problem. She thought of the time when her father was forced to cast a thin, balding, uncertain young man in the part of a backwoods hero in a rousing musical. Henry Speight didn't walk; he crept. He had the look of someone expecting to be attacked from behind. But Henry, a bank teller, had a glorious baritone voice. First, Hap took him to Charleston and bought him a handsome wig. Next, he put him in riding boots, instructing him to wear boots and wig every day from that moment through the run of the play. At first Henry balked, but finally he gave in. In a matter of days, the shrinking teller began to get a new self-image. He looked in the

57

mirror and found a surprisingly attractive face. He couldn't mince in the riding boots, but was forced to stride. His back and shoulders straightened. He no longer dipped his head when he spoke, but, chin lifted, looked everyone in the eye. Suddenly he stood astride his world, in command. Now things were reversed. She had to turn Chance Crown into the original Henry Speight, who, when last heard of, was an anchorman in the Southwest.

When she reached home, she found her mother in the kitchen drinking a glass of milk and paging through a cookbook.

"Where's Milo, Ma?"

"He turned in. The child beat him at six straight games of gin rummy, then sailed to bed. Milo, a defeated man, stumbled off to the barn."

Jervey sat. "How long will he be here?" she asked casually.

"I have no idea. Does it matter?"

"No. I just wondered."

"He's a good friend, Jervey. We remember the same world, laugh at the same things. To the same extent we're full of beans, determined to stick out our tongues at the prospect of old age."

"Sure, Ma."

"He isn't Hap. There'll never be another Hap. But we— well . . ." She closed the cookbook. "How did it go tonight?"

"Good possibilities. Abby will need some help, but—"

"Abby! The great transformation story. Cinderella, Sleeping Beauty, Ugly Duckling."

"What happened to her?"

"Thad Egan. For years she'd worshipped him from afar. I guess, in the long run, Thad realized that utter devotion is a worthy substitute for breathtaking beauty." Roberta finished her milk with one gulp. "Before we knew it, the dormouse, probably using her life savings, took herself to Elizabeth

58

Arden's red something spa and got the full treatment. I must admit they worked miracles."

"Yes. You know, I remember seeing Thad and Elissa Dowell together and thinking most of the women in town are wild about him and most of the men are in love with Elissa. Think of poor old Stanley."

"Oh, Stanley was her slave. Sent flowers to his goddess every month, bought her endless books. With Stanley, I don't think sex came into it. As you may have noticed, Stanley is singularly asexual, a kind of neuter. No, he was obsessive, totally given to daydreaming, worshipping from afar. But when Thad started dating Elissa, Stanley really turned on her. He got very snide about her, passed on bits of gossip with that sly smile. I guess he really was hurt, not entitled to be, but like this great walking wound."

"How about Fred?" asked Jervey.

"Oh, Fred, he used to be the great rebel. Lord, how he swashbuckled to get Elissa's attention, revved up his motorcycle, tried to look sexy and dangerous. When none of that worked, he took a bath and bought a necktie."

"And the mysterious Keith Lynch?"

Roberta walked to the sink, rinsed her glass. "Keith? I haven't a clue."

Jervey rose. "I'm off to bed, Ma." When she reached the door, she turned. "Incidentally, I talked to Sully tonight, asked him about moving the mummy case."

"Did he remember?"

"Finally. But he was pretty mixed up, said the mummy case was wet."

"Wet? But it was in the truck when the fire department came. It didn't get wet."

"Exactly. He's confused."

"But even in an addled state, why would he say it was wet?"

"I haven't a clue," said Jervey.

59

Six

The next night, she went to the theater early and searched the costume room until she found what she needed. Looking at the impressive collection, neatly boxed, marked, and stacked on shelves, she felt a rush of memories. Her schoolgirl uniform from *The Prime of Miss Jean Brodie,* the stunning red satin gown worn by Roberta in *Camille,* the crown worn by Hap when he had to fill in for the king in *Becket.*

She looked at the boxes and could see the actors who'd been so much a part of their lives. Some had died, some had moved away, some were still around. She thought of Hap saying, "The closest thing to the kingdom of heaven is a good cast, no barriers, interdependence, communication, community."

The members of her cast, trained by Hap, were on time, as was Chance Crown, the last to come down the aisle, wearing a crisp, blue shirt, unwrinkled khakis, and, in place of the muddy boots, Indian moccasins. Thad winked at her, and Abby, wearing pale rose Ultrasuede, clutched her script

60

with a sense of purpose. Lotte climbed the steps to the stage, sweating, though the night and the theater were cool. Fred managed a polite nod. Only Stanley looked out of sorts, the coolness of his glance at odds with his grin.

Maybe she'd misread their confidence in her. As they moved through the first act and she broke down scenes, setting changes of relationships, climactic patterns, she sensed a tension that had nothing to do with the play. They all were listening, reacting to her directions, but mechanically. She needed their total concentration. Distraction, she knew, could spread through a cast like a virus. Only Chance seemed wholly present, but his effort to take smaller steps was at odds with the rich authority of his voice, his straight shoulders, the angle of his head.

When they stopped for the coffee break, she led Chance to the men's dressing room. She handed him a pair of black tights and a pair of worn ballet slippers. "I think if you wear these during rehearsals, it might help you."

Chance held up the tights. His eyebrows rose, but he managed to suppress the smallest sign of amusement. "You think they'll fit?" he asked with some skepticism.

"They stretch."

His glance moved to her. "You okay?"

"Sure. Why do you ask that?"

"Everyone seems skittish tonight. Is it always like this? I mean, with plays?"

"Sometimes. This early in rehearsal people are a bit unsure, feeling their way."

"They don't seem unsure to me. I'm doing the doggie paddle in a pool full of Olympic swimmers."

"You're doing fine, Chance."

"But I'm the one who needs the tights." His teeth were a flash of white.

How could she tell him that he was too commanding for the part, too strong, too macho? "Trust me," she said.

She left him in the dressing room and went back on stage where Lotte, Fred, and Thad were sitting together, drinking coffee. Abby sat apart, script open, staring into space. Stanley perched rather primly on a folding chair, as if waiting to be interviewed.

Jervey spent the next few minutes checking her script, the scene they were about to do. "Don't look so glum, Jervey." Thad stood before her. "We won't fail you."

"I know, Thad."

"That young man, Chance, he's not right for the part. We all can see that. As a matter of fact, I thought of calling you today. Bob Sterling is back in town, has a job with Accrolux. Remember Bob? Terrific actor. He did the ailing son in *Long Day's Journey*. He might be willing to—"

The shout from the wings seemed to shake the theater, a cry of triumph and celebration. The figure that leapt from the wings, clad in tights, was larger than life, rising high into the air and landing with splendid balance stage center. There was a communal gasp, followed by startled laughter and then, led by Lotte, a round of applause.

The mysterious tension was broken. Each of them was more relaxed, more willing to concentrate. Jervey sensed that time had given the original cast a wider frame of reference in dealing with emotions and relationships. As they worked through the second act, she saw that they were realizing the dichotomy in their roles. Thad was playing tyranny but, at moments, compassion. Lotte exposed a selfishness in the mother. Stanley found in the oily manipulator a thread of self-hatred. Even Abby, finally abandoning her hard-won savoir-faire, was beginning to find the troubled daughter. Fred's arrogance, blunted by time, was beginning to resound in his character, like a haunting echo. Only Chance, his

62

beautifully muscled legs quite at home in tights, looked not the broken, shadowy Tim, but someone, who at a moment's notice, could replace Baryshnikov.

By the end of rehearsal everyone was tired but in a cheerful mood. Fred stepped in front of her as she was picking up her script and purse. "You know something?"

"What, Fred?"

"You're good." With this brief observation he turned and hurried down the aisle.

"Jervey"—Thad took her arm, his glance moving from Abby, across the stage, to her—"there's something I'd like to talk to you about. Do you suppose we could have lunch one day?"

"Sure, Thad," she agreed, alert with curiosity.

"Day after tomorrow? I'll pick you up around one."

"Fine. I'd like that."

He was about to say more when Abby hurried to his side, put her arm through his. "Ready, darling?"

Jervey watched them leave the theater, baffled by Thad's invitation. It occurred to her, for a heart-stopping moment, that he wanted to drop out of the play. But he wouldn't wait another day to tell her. Could there be trouble in the cast, something she should be told?

Lotte started to leave, then turned to Jervey. "Jervey, I worry about poor old Sully." Her voice was low, confidential. "He seemed so upset last night. What on earth was he talking about?"

"Nothing important, Lotte. He's all right."

"So handicapped. And all alone. He's still living in that rattrap?"

"Yes. But he seems happy enough. Pretty much the same as always."

Lotte shook her head. Pulling a multicolored cape around her shoulders, she clambered down the steps to the aisle.

63

"Stanley?" Jervey stopped him as he came downstage.

"Yes?" His face, a rather grim mask, was transformed at once by an ingratiating smile.

"Is everything okay, Stanley? You're doing a good job. Your part really is coming together."

"You're too nice to me, Jervey. I've got a long way to go. I wish I was a better actor, but I do my best. I mean the others are so professional. You know, you look great, Jervey. One of these days we'll see your name in lights. You—"

"Stanley, if there's anything that bothers you, I hope you'll tell me."

"Sure, I will. You really look great, Jervey. You—well, see you tomorrow night."

He eased away, hurried from the theater. She walked down the aisle into the lobby, stopped in the office to get the cake she'd forgotten the night before. She looked at the fancy box. Lotte was right; it was a bit coy.

"You can't walk home alone with that big box."

She'd thought Chance had left, but there he stood, bigger than life. He'd changed back into his khakis and moccasins and without waiting for her response took the box.

They rode down the main street in his rather muddy red pickup truck. Chance was silent and she felt no impulse, no southern-lady obligation, to initiate a conversation. She thought of the Sunday gatherings of Jason's cognoscenti. She was certain Chance Crown wasn't waiting until he had something meaningful to say. It was a comfortable silence.

It wasn't until she saw the light in Sully's window above the abandoned store that she spoke. "Chance, wait. Can we stop here?"

He didn't ask why, simply pulled over to the curb.

"Sully would love this cake. I won't be a minute."

He followed her down the narrow alley between the two buildings. Beyond was the waterfront park and the harbor.

64

Lights shone on the dock and from some of the boats. There was no doorbell, no knocker on the peeling surface. She rapped loudly. Chance stared toward the water and the open sea beyond. Jervey knocked again.

The door opened with a rush. The big form was in shadow. "Jervey?" The flat dullness of the voice turned rapturous. "Jervey!"

"And this is Chance Crown, Sully. He's in the play. We brought you some cake." There was no need to explain the delivery of cake at eleven-thirty at night. Sully didn't live by clocks. She handed him the box.

"Cake, Jervey! Will you come and have coffee and we'll eat the cake?" He thrust a huge paw in the direction of Chance. "I'm very pleased to meet you, Mr. Chance."

"We can't come in now, Sully. It's late. My mother will worry. Another time."

"Thank you, Jervey. Thank you for the cake. I love cake. You come another time?"

"I will, Sully. Promise. Good night."

Sully, a huge shadow in the doorway, watched them start down the alley. "Jervey!" he yelled suddenly.

She turned. "Yes, Sully?"

"I still got the little trucks you give me, the blue and yellow, and the book with the house and the man on the horse."

When they sat again in the truck, she turned to Chance, tears in her eyes. "I gave him those toys almost twenty years ago."

The downstairs windows of the Parmalee house glowed with light. Jervey surprised herself by inviting Chance to come in for a drink. She expected him to refuse, considering the hour, but he accepted at once. Before they reached the front door she stopped him. "Listen, there's something you have to understand. My mother tends to exaggerate."

65

"She does?"

"Sometimes, usually in a good cause, she lies. Milo is not a millionaire and, as far as I know, has no interest in wildlife or conservation. He's someone Ma met acting in regional theater, probably jobless at the moment and needing a place to roost."

"I see."

She stopped again before unlocking the door, hesitated, then made herself speak. "Chance, why did you agree to be in the play?"

He regarded her with some surprise. His gaze never wavered. For a few seconds he frowned in concentration, then his face cleared. "I want my moment in the limelight?" he suggested. Deadpan, he continued. "No, I guess you don't buy that. How about I'm a shy, insecure person groping for a new image, a confidence that will help me take my place in the world and pursue my impossible dream."

"Confidence to face the challenge of gulls and pelicans?"

"You'd be surprised how tough some of those birds are."

They found Roberta and Milo at the kitchen table, which seemed to be covered with old Parmalee Players programs and newsletters. Neither seemed surprised to see Chance. Roberta made space for him to sit beside her. Jervey introduced Milo, who got them each a beer.

"Ma"—Jervey sank into a chair—"what are you doing with all these programs at this hour?"

Roberta pulled off her glasses. "Trying to find out something about the mysterious Keith Lynch. Those damn bones."

"Ma, I thought we were just playing a game."

"Maybe, at first. But it's been keeping me awake nights."

Milo glanced at Chance. "Perhaps you'd like to know what this is all about."

Chance smiled. "I hate to pry."

66

"Tell him, Ma."

Roberta explained the finding of the bones, the hearing aid, the various movings of the mummy case, the cast of the original *The Spelling of Honour,* the mysterious Keith, who, his car packed for departure, supposedly left after the play.

Chance listened attentively. "I suppose there could be other explanations for the bones," he said.

"Yes," Jervey spoke quickly.

"We haven't told you everything," Roberta addressed Jervey. "Today I talked to people from theater groups in Charlotte, Charleston, and Abbeville. They all said Keith Lynch hadn't been in plays with them."

"So?" Jervey suppressed a yawn.

"About nine o'clock tonight I got a call back from the Footlight Players in Charleston. The director had talked to an actor who remembered that Keith Lynch had been cast in *The Subject Was Roses* but had to drop out. He'd had an accident. Skiing in North Carolina. Broke his leg."

"Ma, look—"

"Milo and I went up to the attic and looked again at those bones."

"I hope you didn't take Emma."

"One of the leg bones," said Milo, "shows distinct signs of a fracture or break."

No one spoke for several seconds. "Not enough to call in the law," said Chance, "but it sure makes you wonder."

Jervey had a cold feeling in the pit of her stomach. She refused to acknowledge a growing conviction that something unspeakable had happened on a closing night ten years ago. It filled her with dread, sickened her to think of the desecration of Hap's theater, where the closest thing to the kingdom of heaven was a good cast.

"One thing I wonder about," said Chance. "If that box—

67

mummy case—was stored in your barn with a decaying body inside, wouldn't someone have gotten a whiff of it?"

"Yes," Milo agreed. "It would have been pretty strong."

Roberta rose and walked to the sink, stared out the window at the darkness, broken only by a distant streetlight. "I thought of that myself, then I remembered that *The Spelling of Honour* was the last play of the season. Two days after it closed Hap, Jervey, and I went to England for a month, then Ireland for a month. Remember, Jervey, we didn't get back until September."

"Still . . ." Milo persisted.

"I think you're forgetting how far that barn is from the house."

"Was the barn kept locked at all times?" asked Milo.

"Padlocked."

"It's all so crazy," Jervey insisted. "Why would anyone kill that man and then put him in the mummy case?" She realized that she was the first one to come out and say that the bones could be the remains of Keith Lynch.

"Maybe they didn't have time to do otherwise." Milo rubbed his chin. "Maybe they stashed the body intending to come back later and dispose of it."

"Yes." Roberta returned to the table. "And then there was the fire that night. If they came back before the fire, the case probably was already in the truck. If they came after the fire, they'd assume it had been burned."

"So the murderer," said Milo, "whether he checked earlier or not would have returned to find only ashes and debris, figured he was home free."

"Oh, God!" Roberta closed her eyes. "I can't believe we're sitting here, making conjectures about a murder in our own theater, committed by someone we might know."

"Not necessarily, Ma. Someone could have wandered in

68

after everyone went to the cast party, found Keith still there, and decided to rob him. When he resisted—"

She stopped and stared at the doorway where Emma, hair on end, looking like a waif in her oversize T-shirt nightgown, regarded them solemnly. "I woke up and heard voices," she said. She rubbed her eyes. "Frankly, I think it was an inside job." She walked over and stood beside Jervey. Her voice was hopeful. "Is anyone having something to eat?"

Seven

· · · · · ·

Jervey woke up at first light. Emma slept soundly beside her, mouth slightly open. Trying not to wake the child, she slid out of bed, put on a jogging suit, bright pink, pulled on socks and shoes, and crept downstairs.

When she stepped outside she could feel autumn in the air, the first crisp chill. The leaves were starting to turn and soon would be falling, carpeting the quiet streets. She loved the town at this hour, the utter if deceptive peace. She wondered if Chance Crown already was steering his boat along a river or creek, checking the wildlife, looking for poachers. As she started to jog down the empty street, she thought of him leaping from the wings and landing stage center. She found herself laughing out loud. She had to admit that he was an attractive man in a very offbeat way. One minute he talked like a yokel who'd grown up in the swamps and the next minute like a person of education and background. Without effort he seemed always in control. She'd never caught him off balance. He took everything in stride, even his flaws as an

70

actor. As Thad said, Chance was all wrong for the part of Tim.

By the time she reached the north end of the waterfront park, the sun was bright. A few people moved on the dock. A charter boat with six aspiring fishermen started toward the mouth of the harbor and the open sea. Gulls flung themselves at a silvery pink sky and swooped toward the dock looking for scraps. She jogged to the south end of the park and then onto the open beach, stopping to pick up a shell for Emma. Jogging, whether it was on the Upper West Side of New York or in Oldport, always removed her from her current problems. She managed to feel disengaged, to observe herself from a distance. Not today. She kept seeing the damn bones in the mummy case, the accruing bits of evidence that something was awry. Despite the fact that the hearing aid and the sign of a broken leg could be coincidence, she had a gut feeling that something ominous was being thrust upon them.

Finally she had to admit that she was tired, retraced her path on the beach to the park, and turned up a narrow passage to the main street. She saw cars, people, signs of early-morning activity. It was several minutes before she realized that a number of cars had stopped, the drivers looking hesitantly ahead where a crowd was gathered on the street and sidewalk. For a few seconds no one was moving, then an old man pulled a gray-haired woman from the group and led her away. A paper boy, craning to see, fell from his bike, scattering papers.

She saw where the crowd had gathered. By some instinctive subconscious connection, she knew. She ran, already breathless, feeling that she moved in slow motion, thrusting herself toward something she was terrified to face.

First she saw strangers, then Cobb Raines, who owned the drugstore. Bob Sherrill, who ran the gas station, was pushing people back. Lotte, wild-eyed, gaped at her. She saw Thad, Abby burying her face on his shoulder.

71

Sully, like a huge broken doll, lay on the sidewalk, awash with blood, arms spread, legs at odd angles, his head crushed.

"Sully!" The cry tore from her throat. It parted the crowd. She threw herself forward, fell to the sidewalk. With a ragged sob she pulled the bloody head into her lap. There was a hush, like a drawn sigh, then the sound of voices, muted, shocked. Someone was beside her. Thad had his hands on her shoulders, but she pulled away and tried to cradle the dead man.

"Sully," she crooned softly as if to reassure him. "Oh, Sully." She stared into his wide, glazed eyes, felt his blood seep through her shirt.

Suddenly, stronger hands pulled the body from her lap. She cried out, struggled. She felt herself being carried, borne past the stunned faces, heard someone say, "He fell from the doorway up there, poor devil." She heard the sound of sirens. She closed her eyes and felt Chance lift her into the truck.

Curled up, arms around her legs, she could feel rough, grainy leather under her cheek. She tried to tell herself that she'd not yet gotten out of bed, was just waking from a bad dream. Not until she was being bounced, shaken, did she force herself to lift her head. She saw the dashboard, then, below, the muddy boots. She saw Chance, hands on the steering wheel, staring straight ahead.

She pulled herself up, swung her feet to the floor of the truck. She, too, stared straight ahead. It was as if some giant hand mercifully had wiped out all feeling. She felt weightless, suspended. She looked at the tall pines on either side, the rutted dirt road. She had no idea of how long she'd been in the truck. She was sure she'd never seen the narrow road before. But there was a lot of land around Oldport she'd never seen. During her childhood there had been few country excursions. Life had centered around the old Victorian homestead and the Parmalee Playhouse.

She wondered why she wasn't surprised at Chance's si-

72

lence. Anyone else would have been soothing her with awkward bromides. At last they turned into an even narrower road with taller trees, denser undergrowth. Straight ahead she saw a hut so weatherworn it almost faded into the woods around it. It sat on the curve of a creek or narrow river. There was a small dock and near it an upended canoe.

He parked near the dock, came around, and opened the door on her side. Before she could move, he reached up and lifted her to the ground. The hut was built of wood covered with green tar paper. It had a tin roof and a brick chimney and did not look very inviting. When Chance opened the door she caught her breath. Heart pine walls and floors glowed with a soft polish. A big sofa, dark red, stretched in front of a stone fireplace with deep armchairs on either side. She saw a long table arranged as a desk, brass lamps, three walls of crowded bookshelves. Just beyond was a small kitchen with a window looking toward the river. There were no curtains, no rugs. A large picture of two pelicans in flight hung over the mantel.

He left her to look around and went into a room to the left. When he came back, he carried some clothes, a blue sweater and some jeans.

She spoke at last, her voice weak, as dazed as she felt. "Why did you bring me here?"

He looked first at her face, then his glance moved lower. She looked down at her pink sweatshirt, covered with blood. "Your mother," he said, "the little girl, I thought you'd want to clean up before they saw you."

"Yes." Her mind felt fuzzy. "I'd better call Ma." She headed for the phone on his desk, then stopped, not turning. "Thank you," she said.

Her conversation with her mother was brief. Roberta had answered sleepily, still unaware of what had happened. She

73

didn't ask where Jervey was and Jervey hung up without explaining.

She showered for a long time in the tiny bathroom. When she returned to the living room, she was enveloped in the big, blue sweater and sagging rolled-up jeans, her hair in wet curls. Chance regarded her solemnly, hands on his hips. Then he grinned.

He didn't press her to eat a big breakfast. She sat on the sofa and he put a small table beside her. She drank strong coffee, managed a piece of toast, stared at the picture of the pelicans. "You a photographer?" she asked.

"In my off-hours. I have a darkroom behind the bedroom back there."

"I know practically nothing about you."

"You know I should be with the New York City Ballet, not buried in a one-horse town."

She found herself smiling. She realized he was waiting to see if she was ready to talk about what had happened. She wasn't.

"What did you do before you were a conservation officer?"

"I tried business. The restaurant business, the Charleston tour business, even big business. Had a job with Accrolux. By the time they offered me a raise I knew I had no business in the world of business. Besides, I was having trouble breathing. When this job became available, I grabbed it."

"Any regrets?"

"About dying and going to heaven?" He took her coffee cup and went to refill it. When he handed back the cup he sat beside her. "What about you, Jervey?"

"I suppose I had what you'd call a good childhood, never dull, that's for sure." She found it a relief to be talking.

"After college?"

"I went to New York, tried to be an actress. I'm still trying,

74

I guess. I've done some parts off Broadway, a few film bits. Doing two TV ads really saved the day, pays the bills."

"You don't sound fired up with ambition."

She looked at him, looked away. "Theater in New York is a far cry from what my father taught and practiced. When you mention craft up there, everyone looks through you. And getting a part, it's hit or miss, who you know, Russian roulette. The directors, actors—well there don't seem to be many real pros, as my father would call them. Only innovators."

"You seem to be doing a damn good job of directing."

She looked at him carefully. "You really think so?"

"Jervey, you handle people with amazing skill, get across your ideas, change, shape, lead without ever stepping on a toe. You've taught me one helluva lot."

She felt herself beginning to blush, rose quickly, and carried her cup and plate to the kitchen. From the window she could see ducks flying down and settling on the water. Then just beyond, between a stand of trees and the river, a young deer appeared. It stood motionless, head lifted.

"Chance, look!"

She waited until he was beside her. They watched the deer move carefully, tentatively toward the water, stopping twice to lift its head, sense any possible danger.

"Beautiful," she breathed.

"Yes."

"Chance," she found she was whispering, "that's it, that's Tim, the character. Can you see?"

He leaned toward the window. "Yes." He paused. "I see what you mean now." Together they watched in silence while the deer drank, then turned and disappeared.

It was she who suggested that they drive back to town. She mentioned it with reluctance, not wanting to go. For a brief, fragile time she'd felt safe and oddly free of pain. Sitting again

75

in the truck, she felt the return of tension. He seemed to sense this. He drew her attention to a raccoon observing them from the roadside. He slowed the truck to point out an eagle's nest in a tall pine. No mention was made of Sully, nor was there any verbal attempt to soothe. She was grateful to him.

Roberta opened the door before they reached it. She pulled Jervey into the house and as Chance started back to the truck she spoke to him. "Thank you, Chance. Bless you."

She led Jervey upstairs, closed the door of the bedroom, and put her arms around her. "Sleep, sugar," she whispered. "Sleep knits up the raveled sleeve of everything."

Flung across her bed, still wearing Chance's clothes, Jervey seemed to plunge into sleep. She awoke once, saw Roberta sitting in the rocker by the window, closed her eyes, and slept even more deeply. When she woke again the rocker was empty, but Emma stood by the bed. She looked solemnly at Jervey, started to speak, stopped.

"What time is it, Emma?"

"I don't know. Roberta and Milo are fixing supper. Some lady brought a pie and a venturesome stew."

"Venison stew?"

"Yeah. I think I'll have scrambled eggs."

Jervey got up, took off Chance's clothes, and folded them neatly. She put on her orange robe and, with Emma, went down to the kitchen. Milo had just finished setting the table and Roberta stood stirring something in a large iron pot. As soon as they saw her, they applied quick, cheerful smiles.

"Just in time." Roberta waved the spoon. "Lotte came bearing gifts. That woman must cook all day. Milo, you forgot the napkins. Venison stew and exotic Austro-Hungarian pie, Jervey. Sit down, everybody."

They sat, the four of them, like a carefree family, something from a Hallmark greeting card. Roberta chattered a bit. Milo, watching her anxiously, offered gems from his endless supply of theater anecdotes. They ate little of the delicious stew. Emma shoved her eggs from one side of the plate to the other. After they'd all declined the pie, Jervey pushed away from the table.

Roberta spoke quickly. "You know Hap always loved Key lime pie. And I never got it right. I remember one time where we had guests for dinner and I cut into my latest effort and it looked like—"

"Ma, please shut up!"

They all turned to her in shock. "Really, Jervey—"

"Sully didn't fall from that French door!" Her voice was firm, cold. Something, festering in her subconscious mind, pushed to the surface, erupted. "Sully had stood in that door for years, inviting people to have coffee. I've heard Hap warn him about it, tell him to be careful."

She stood, kicked back her chair, spread her arms. "He held on like this, using one hand to wave. He loved it when people waved back. Dammit, he didn't fall! He was pushed!"

"Jervey"—Roberta made a weak gesture—"the child—"

"Emma's not a baby, Ma. She's seen enough of life not to be sent off to the nursery."

"That's right," piped Emma.

"What makes you so sure, Jervey?" asked Milo.

"The other night, Sully came up to the stage during rehearsal and talked about the mummy case. In front of everyone. He remembered moving it from truck to truck and into the barn. He said he lifted the case alone because he had strong arms."

Her defiant glance moved from face to face. "That mummy case is made of plywood. Empty, I could lift it. What's more, he said it was wet."

"Jervey," Roberta spoke gently, "we know the case was taken from the theater before the fire, before they came in with the hoses. Poor Sully was totally confused."

77

"Maybe," chirped Emma, "the victim was taking a bath. I saw this TV show where a girl was electrocuted when someone threw a hair dryer in the tub."

"There are no tubs in the theater," said Roberta patiently.

"Showers?" suggested Milo.

"Two. Men's and women's bathrooms." Jervey spoke absently, her mind elsewhere.

"Oh my God!" Roberta leaned heavily on the table. "The shower! I remember Hap talking about—he was really amused—this fellow Keith was quite a dandy. He showered and got dressed up after every performance, as if he was going to a party or somewhere. He—" She stopped abruptly.

"Could have been stuffed in that case, soaking wet," finished Milo. "That would explain why there are no remnants of clothing. And with the hole in the mummy case made by the rats, giving insects an entry, it's obvious why only bones are left."

"Is it enough to call the sheriff?" asked Jervey.

Milo shook his head. "I'm afraid not."

"But if someone killed Sully because they thought he knew something—I mean there could be a murderer in this town and we can't just sit here and do nothing!"

"Sully's death will undoubtedly be ruled an accident," said Milo. He turned to her, spoke quietly. "Jervey, we have indications but no hard evidence. None. And if you're getting suspicious of your cast, those people who were in the original production, there's an important question."

"What?" Emma was riveted.

"Suppose one of them is guilty, why would he or she be willing to blithely return to the scene of the crime, same theater, same play, almost the same cast?"

"Ma, was anyone reluctant to be in the play again? Come on, tell the truth. I know your powers of persuasion."

Roberta picked up a spoon, regarded it with interest. "They all were."

"All!"

"Well, Thad gave me a flat no, said he was swamped with work. A day later, I saw Abby at the mall and told her we'd hoped she'd play the part of the daughter, a fat role, as you know. I could tell she was flattered, tempted. She'd never played anything but bits. But she hemmed and hawed. That night, Thad called and said they'd decided to help out. Lotte was not enthusiastic, told me she might have to be out of town during the run. When I stretched the truth and told her the rest of the cast was raring to go and that I'd understudy her part, she agreed. Stanley oiled around about how flattered he was to be asked, whined a bit about the length of the part and his problem learning lines but eventually he—"

"Fred?"

Roberta pondered, put down the spoon. "You know, I don't remember."

When Jervey sighed, Roberta spoke up quickly, as if to compensate for her lack of total recall. "I do remember one thing. Ten years ago, after the first rehearsal of the play, Hap came home, had a stiff drink, and told me he had a great cast but they were going to be hell on wheels."

"What did he mean?" Emma asked.

"He meant personality problems, conflicts, competitiveness, jealousy, insecurity both on- and offstage."

"Was he right, Ma?"

"He never mentioned it again. I guess he ironed things out, kept control."

Jervey sat numbly, unwilling to believe she had a murderer in her cast yet certain that Sully had been pushed to his death. She made herself move. "I'm going upstairs to work on the script for a while."

Roberta looked at her with concern. "You could call off tonight's rehearsal. I can phone everyone and—"

"No."

Roberta, Milo, and Emma insisted on doing the dishes, after which they planned to go to the library and watch a Masterpiece Theatre play on TV. Jervey went to her room and sat on the bed going over her script. She told herself she was checking to see if she had set the climactic patterns, marked what Hap called the "frissons." It dawned on her that she was not thinking as a director but looking for direction. She was squinting at Hap's symbolic notes on the actors or their characters at the back of the script when Emma wandered in, crawled on the bed beside her.

"You didn't like the play, Emma?"

"Not enough action. What do those funny little pictures mean?" She was pointing to the symbols Hap had drawn by the name of each cast member.

"I'm not sure."

"Thad has a crown," noted Emma, "Lotte a rectangle, Stanley two masks—"

"A Janus," said Jervey, "two-faced."

"Fred a snake—"

"Or an eel."

"Elissa a ball."

"Or an egg. And Keith a knife. I think my father used those symbols as a key to character."

Emma studied them, tracing each with a grubby finger. "In real life or in the play?"

When she walked to the playhouse that night, Jervey felt no apprehension, only a sense of loss. Losing Sully was losing a part of her life. Sully, reaching out, asked only to share a cup of coffee with the world.

Thad and Abby arrived first, looking at Jervey a bit hesitantly but then seemed to be reassured by her calmness.

80

"Jervey," Thad's eyes seemed to reflect her own grief, "honey, I'm sorry you had to be there this morning. Lord, I really am sorry about that."

Abby sank into a chair. Her voice was small. "Such a shock. Thad was out jogging. He had a call, some legal SOS from the office. I drove out to find him. When I turned down Main Street . . ." Her voice dwindled away.

Lotte climbed the steps to the stage. She brought no pastry. She looked older, even her draperies drooping. She squeezed Jervey's arm, moved across the stage, and plugged in the coffee machine.

Stanley and Fred arrived together. Fred's right eye was swollen. A ragged bandage hung loosely on his jaw. At Jervey's questioning look, he grinned. "A difference of opinion at the Blue Dolphin." He paused beside her. "Listen, I'm sorry about what happened to the old guy."

"Thank you, Fred."

He continued to stand beside her, chewing his lip, until Stanley moved in. For once, Stanley was not obsequious. He held her hand between both of his for a few seconds. Somehow, he looked taller, his eyes less watery. He looked at her with real concern, as if for the moment he'd forgotten himself.

She watched him walk over and join Lotte. She glanced at the aisle, waiting for Chance, then remembered he was not scheduled to come that night.

The rehearsal was not brilliant but better than she'd expected. She herself was more incisive in her directions. She showed Lotte how to physically dramatize recalling her girlhood by moving like an adolescent, then coming back to the present as an arthritic older woman. She added moments of hesitation to Thad's portrayal of arrogance to show the character for a moment thrown off balance by his own smooth tyranny. Stanley seemed to grasp what she meant when she

81

told him that the audience must, at first, be ambivalent about his character, torn between sympathy and distrust.

Only Fred was unreceptive, going through the scenes mechanically, line perfect but oddly distracted. From time to time he touched his livid eye, pawed at the bandage on his jaw.

She knew they all were trying to be helpful, quickly adapting to new directions. Even Fred rallied finally. She was aware that each of them was watching her with careful concentration as if at any moment she might fall apart.

Eight

Jervey and Roberta made plans for Sully's funeral. He had no family. He would be buried in the Parmalee plot in St. George's churchyard. Father Jake Barnham would conduct a graveside service the next day.

Early that morning Milo, looking like a British baronet, had taken off in the Bentley to visit friends in Charleston.

"I admit he's rather fetching, Ma," said Jervey. "Is he on vacation? Having a run of bad luck?"

"He's not had an easy life." Roberta wore a pair of Hap's pajamas, over which she'd absently thrown a raincoat.

"Has he ever been married?"

"Jervey, what is this? Are you concerned that a city slicker will take advantage of your poor witless mumsy? Yes, he's been married." Roberta spoke grudgingly, as if forced. "She was an actress named Laura. They both did stage, TV, films. They toured, the two of them, doing scenes from the classics, largely for colleges, clubs. It was a good marriage, a special marriage. She died eight years ago."

"Are there any muffins left?" Emma stood in the kitchen doorway looking both hopeful and apprehensive.

"My God!" Roberta almost dropped her cup. "What have you done to yourself?"

"I trimmed my hair." Emma, glasses askew, peered at them coolly.

"Emma!" Jervey started to rise, dropped back in her chair.

"Trimmed!" Roberta regarded the almost-shorn head, tufts of red hair sticking out at odd angles.

"All that fuzz. It was driving me ape."

Roberta rose with deliberation. "Come with me." She led the child out of the room and up the steps.

Jervey stood at the kitchen window, looking out at the unkempt garden. No Parmalee seemed to have a green thumb. A bird feeder atop a listing pole was being investigated by a hungry applicant who refused to believe there was no seed. She remembered when Hap had brought home the feeder, dug a hole, thrust the pole into the ground, and poured seed from a big bag. The next morning she and Hap had stood at that same window and watched a large, feathered creature alight on the birdhouse.

"What is it?" Jervey had asked. "A raven?"

"Well," Hap had mulled this over for a few seconds, "I don't think so. Maybe a very small vulture or a very big wren."

"Oh."

"But that," announced Hap confidently as a tiny creature approached the pole, "is undeniably a squirrel."

Thad Egan called to confirm that she would join him for lunch. They agreed that he would pick her up at twelve-thirty. She found herself much too concerned about what to wear. Did one ever get over girlhood crushes? She remembered herself as a teenager, walking down Main Street, hoping to see Thad. When he was in a play she'd sit through

84

endless rehearsals. The day Hap died of a heart attack, Thad arrived within hours, helped Roberta with funeral arrangements, opened the door to the throngs of people who stopped by to pay respects. Quiet, strong, always tactful, he guided them through the whole week of grief, confusion, decisions.

She went to the library and finally found a *Book of Common Prayer,* wedged between *Costumes of the Eighteenth Century* and *The Complete Plays of Noel Coward,* and picked out some prayers for Sully's funeral. All of them seemed too formal for that most uncomplicated man.

Roberta entered the library with a flourish. She'd shed the raincoat and rolled up the pajama sleeves. She wore a look of great self-satisfaction. "Voilà!" She pushed Emma into the room.

The red mane was now a cap of shiny close-cut curls. The face looked less round, eyes larger, the chin pointed, rather elfin.

"What's more," Roberta admired her handiwork, "she doesn't really need those awful glasses. She was able to read a whole page of *Who's Who in Theater* without them."

"I have this friend," said Emma airily, "who goes to the Piero Medici Salon every week to have her hair styled, nails manicured, and legs waxed."

"Indeed," said Roberta drily.

"Emma, you're gorgeous," said Jervey.

Emma actually blushed, was aware of it, and a bit mortified. "Look," she said casually, "I'm going down to Main Street for a while, have to get a few things. Any errands?"

"Do you need some money?" asked Jervey.

"No."

"Run along," said Roberta, "and dazzle the locals."

When Jervey told Roberta about her lunch date with Thad that day, Roberta shook her head, laughed. "Good old Thad. He must think you have problems."

"Ma, I'm going to ask him what happened ten years ago, about the cast, what was going on. I think he'd be honest with me."

"It wouldn't hurt to ask."

But a few hours later, sitting with Thad in a chic new restaurant south of the town, she asked him nothing. Mostly, she listened. To avoid gaping raptly at the elegant bone structure of his face, she looked out the window at the expanse of marsh.

"I just wanted to make sure you're okay, Jervey." He spoke softly, almost apologetically. "And I've been concerned about the play. It's a helluva burden for those young shoulders. And now, what happened with Sully—I wouldn't blame you if you stood up and let out a primal scream."

"I'm all right, Thad."

"Sure?"

"Sure."

"Any ideas about a replacement for Chance Crown? I can still call that fellow I told you about, sound him out, at least."

"Let's give Chance a little longer, Thad. He might surprise us."

"I don't want him to be too much of a surprise for you, Jervey."

She let herself look at him directly, indulged herself in the warmth of his gaze. "What do you mean?"

He leaned back in his chair, frowned, then canceled the frown with a quick smile. "You've always trusted people, Jervey; from the time you were young I can remember the wide-eyed trust in that face. It was daunting. Hap worried about you. I worry about you."

"Should I distrust Chance Crown?"

"I didn't say that."

"You implied it." She was aware of a quickened heartbeat.

86

"Jervey, I'm not a gossip. I loathe gossip, people spreading stories, unsubstantiated, often vicious—"

"About Chance? Thad, what are you getting at? If there's something I should know . . ."

"All I'm asking is that you proceed with caution." He reached out, covered her hand with his. "I'm damned if I'll see you hurt."

"Thad—"

"No, I'm not going to say any more."

He didn't. He led her into a discussion of the play, managed not only to distract her but to make her laugh. At one point, she almost told him about the bones in the attic, her suspicion about Sully's death, but she didn't. When he left her at her front door, she felt guilty for not confiding in him.

That night's rehearsal showed that Chance had given a lot of thought to his part. He still was too strong a personality, but he'd begun to soften the edges, speak with less obvious authority. The tights and ballet slippers were having an effect. His steps were smaller, his movements slower, more deliberate.

Jervey was disturbed by her personal reactions to Chance. Hap, in his theater lingo, would say she was moving both toward and away from him, trying to affirm his efforts with the part on one hand and backing off on the other. At the end of the rehearsal he handed her the pink jogging suit, washed and folded.

"Chance, I meant to bring the clothes you loaned me. I forgot."

"That's all right. Can I give you a lift home?"

"Stanley's taking me. But, thanks."

Roberta once had told her that you can learn a lot about a man by the car he drives. It may not reflect his personality but, very often, his self-image. As she climbed into Stanley's fairly new Cadillac she knew her mother could be wrong.

Stanley's car reflected neither the pale obsequious personality nor the cringing self-image.

"Jervey, I thought that, maybe—well, I know you're probably tired, but I was wondering if you might like—now, you be frank, but I thought we might stop at the Blue Dolphin for a drink."

"I'd like that, Stanley."

The popular Blue Dolphin, housed in a one-story cinder-block building at the north end of Main Street, aimed to look like a pub. Hunting prints hung on the brick-faced walls, the lighting fixtures resembled carriage lamps, and the long bar of polished wood had a brass foot rail.

As on most weeknights, the bar was not crowded. Stanley, holding Jervey's arm, led her across the dimly lit room to a booth near the back. He was pathetically pleased, getting her settled with something of a flourish.

"Jervey, I'm so glad you came. I've been wanting to—well, we've known each other for a long time but I never—"

"I'm glad you asked me, Stanley."

"I'll get you a drink. What would you like?"

"A beer would be fine."

She watched him move to the bar with a sense of purpose, give the order, then wait with a mixture of pleasure and impatience. She wondered how life had made him so self-effacing, so unsure of himself. She knew little about him except that he'd never married, lived with his sister, and worked in a lab at Accrolux. Before that he'd been involved in a kitchen-equipment store that folded. One night he'd invited Hap and Roberta to his house for a drink after rehearsal. Roberta was amused by the fact that the dining room table already was set with two places for breakfast. None of them had ever met the sister.

"I hope you like this brand, Jervey." He put the can of beer and a glass in front of her. "I'll get some chips and nuts, but if you're really hungry maybe you'd like—"

"Stanley, I'm fine. Do sit down."

He sat, took a sip of his drink, watched Jervey pour beer into her glass. "Jervey, I'm so sorry about Sully."

"I know, Stanley."

"He was such a harmless fellow. Didn't have much of a life, did he?"

"No. But he didn't realize that."

"Like a little kid."

"Yes."

"Lotte told me what happened. She was out walking. She walks every morning. She ran into Thad and they went on together. When they turned into Main Street, they saw the crowd."

"I saw them."

"Lotte's really something else." He half grinned. "I'll bet she's had quite a life."

"Probably."

The watery blue eyes had a look of sly amusement. "When you ask about her past, she really clams up."

Suddenly, out of the blue, two thoughts hit her, Stanley's love of gossip and the fact that he knew far more about the cast members than she. Also, it was impossible to imagine Stanley killing someone and putting them in a prop mummy case.

"Stanley, my mother and I are really upset about something."

"You are?" She could see, feel his curiosity.

"Something we found, some things that look terribly suspicious. Actually, it's pretty damn frightening."

He was all ears. "Frightening, Jervey?"

In the end, she told him everything. She watched his eyes

89

widen. He sat deathly still. When she got to her suspicions about Sully's death, he seemed to shrink into himself.

"But what you're suggesting—" he whispered.

"I know. I don't want to believe it myself. But there are too many coincidences, Stanley. They keep hitting us over the head."

He said nothing. She leaned in, her arms on the table. "Stanley, I wish you'd think back to that first production, all of you in the cast."

"You believe someone in the cast—"

"I don't know what to think. The only people in the theater that night after the show were the cast. The men, as you know, doubled as crew. Abby was stage manager. Stanley, were there any bad feelings in the cast? Was it a good cast?"

"Oh, we were good," Stanley said quickly. He stared at his drink, then looked at her with a pleased expression. "Hap didn't say so, but we could tell."

"Was it a happy cast?" He seemed reluctant to answer. "What about Keith Lynch, Stanley?"

The answer was immediate, harsh. "He was a troublemaker from the beginning."

She said nothing, waited.

Stanley stammered, then spoke quickly, almost compulsively. "He acted by himself, very vain if you ask me. Thad tried to draw him into things, took him out for drinks, talked to him a lot during coffee breaks. But he was a loner. A loner."

"What about Fred and Keith?"

"Oh, Fred." The half grin reappeared. "Fred had been making a big play for Elissa. Of course she was nice to him, nice to everybody. But, Fred! He even wore an earring then, like some leftover hippie. One night"—he leaned in, lowered

90

his voice—"he and Keith almost came to blows in the dressing room."

"What about?"

"I don't know. I was in the wings, checking my props. But I could hear their voices. By the time I got there, Thad had stopped them. You can bet Fred was jealous of Keith and Elissa!"

"It seems to me that if Thad was dating Elissa, he should have been the jealous one."

"They weren't dating. They were seen together, sure, but they weren't dating. I think she was going through some kind of personal crisis, something to do with defying her father. Thad was trying to help her."

"Abby?"

He didn't answer. He was staring at nothing.

"Abby?"

"Oh." He looked at her, shook his head. "Who knows about Abby? She was certainly different back then, a real ugly duckling. Being married to Thad's sure made a difference. I guess she was attracted to Keith because he was so good-looking, a real pretty boy. You know the type, the face of a choirboy and the heart of a con man."

"You think he was dishonest?"

"I didn't say that. No, he used people. And he was a drifter. Any woman who got mixed up with him was in for—he was bad news. He was—"

"Lotte?"

"They left rehearsal together several times." His face brightened at a sudden memory. "Twice I saw her giving him money. Once I got to the theater early, saw them backstage, her handing him some bills. Another time was here, in that booth over there. She was counting out some cash."

"Did she look upset?"

91

Stanley thought about it. "No," he said, "but she looked kind of, well, secret."

She thought about her father's observation that the cast was "hell on wheels." She looked at Stanley, so pleased to be having a drink with her, so willing to tell her everything. He was a born gossip.

"Stanley, let's keep all this between you and me."

"You can count on it, Jervey."

Nine

There were over a hundred people to say good-bye to Sully—church members, storekeepers who were Sully's neighbors, the cast of *The Spelling of Honour,* and a number of other Parmalee Players. They stood among the drifting leaves in the small churchyard. The air was cool and the late-afternoon sun moved through the massive oaks.

The casket Roberta and Jervey had chosen was suspended above the open grave. Father Jake Barnham stood, prayer book in hand, his face not solemn but lit, as always, with his particular joy. As he addressed them, his gaze moved from one person to another.

"We come together today to affirm our belief that a friend is safe in God's hands. We cannot mourn that. What we do mourn is our own loss, the departure of a loving, innocent man who was part of our lives. We all remember Sully waving from his window. I think that somewhere he still waves to each of us."

Jervey tightened her fists to hold back the tears. She looked across the crowd and saw the members of the cast, except for Chance, standing together.

"I am the resurrection and the life, saith the Lord: he that believeth in me, though he were dead, yet shall he live . . ."

She heard the ancient words of comfort as Father Jake went through the service. She stared at the cast. Each seemed somehow shrunken, diminished. Her thoughts were scattered, irrelevant. She'd never seen Fred in a suit before. Lotte seemed haggard, a handkerchief pressed to her mouth. Thad and Abby held hands. Stanley pulled himself stiffly erect. None of them looked like a murderer.

"The Lord is my light and my salvation . . ."

She saw Chance on the edge of the crowd, standing inches taller than anyone else. Except for the thick, unstyled hair, he looked like a junior executive. His eyes were fixed in her direction. She felt as if she were waiting all alone in the falling leaves, confused, torn, and filled with a creeping fear. Then she felt Emma's hand, finding hers.

The service drew to an end; the casket had been lowered. She was aware of people beginning to move. But Father Jake was not quite finished. His strong voice rang out.

"Whoever receives this child in my name receives me."

Roberta had to speak to her twice before Jervey heard her. "Are you ready to go, dear?"

"You all go ahead," said Jervey. "I'd like to walk home."

"If you're sure."

"I'm sure."

She watched Roberta, Milo, and Emma walk toward the street where the car was parked. She watched people turn and move away. Two men were shoveling dirt into the grave. Jake Barnham came toward her. For once his look of joy was dimmed by concern. He held out his arms. Head on his shoulder, eyes closed, she let herself rest there. "God love you," he said quietly.

94

She could have stayed forever in that strong embrace, but Lotte was beside her, taking her arm. "Jervey, come with Fred and me. We're going back to my house for a drink. Come."

Before she could agree or decline, she was led away between Lotte and Fred. She sat numbly in the blue Honda as they drove to the south end of town. Later, she remembered wondering if Fred was really a Honda or if that was his self-image.

Lotte's small two-storied frame house was in need of paint. One shutter sagged and the mailbox by the picket fence looked about to fall. But the grass, shrubs, and small flowerbeds were well tended. The front door led into the living room and an overpowering smell of cats. A huge tabby sprawled on a window seat amid a mess of newspapers and magazines, a Siamese hissed from its perch on the upright piano, and two mangy-looking Angoras slept on the sagging sofa, blending into the faded floral chintz.

"Sit, dear," commanded Lotte, sweeping the cats from the sofa. "Fred, you, too. I'll get us a little grog."

She sat on the sofa, facing Fred, who slumped into an enormous armchair. He had a peeled, exposed look, his dark, oily hair pulled tightly into a pigtail. His suit seemed too small for him. He stared down at his worn suede shoes as if seeing them for the first time.

"Fred," she heard herself saying, "I've been meaning to tell you how well you're doing with your part." Oh, Lord, she thought, Hap wouldn't have said that. Hap's compliments were rare and oblique. "It's not an easy part," she went on, "all those changes, contradictions." She knew she was trying to get a response, any response. "Is it easier doing it this time?"

His gaze moved from his shoes to the window. "It is and it isn't. The mechanics are easier because I've played more

95

parts. In another way it's tougher because I know more about what makes people tick."

It was the most she'd ever heard him say. Fred always had been a closed person, even to Hap. An enigma, someone who read well at tryouts, performed well during the run, and then disappeared until he chose to show up for another tryout.

"I see what you mean."

"That's a good-looking suit, Jervey. Green's a good color on you. An' I've never seen you in high heels before. A woman's legs look better in high heels."

"I guess so."

"Do you like jazz?"

"Sure."

"There's this little place up the coast . . ." his voice ebbed.

"Have you lived here long, Fred? I mean, were you born here?"

"Born or reborn?" He giggled suddenly, watching her, pleased with himself.

"Here we are!" Lotte strode into the room bearing a tray of thick mugs. The three of them sat in a companionable arrangement, Lotte beside Jervey on the sofa. Two more cats, yellow, with bristly fur, trailed in. Lotte got up to turn on a tape and a Mahler symphony swelled around them. They sipped their drinks, hot cider laced with something much stronger.

It was not really companionable. For some reason the air was thick with tension. Lotte sprawled, but there was a stiffness to her shoulders. Fred sat forward in the armchair, holding his mug between his knees. Hap would be able to read the body language, Jervey told herself. Why am I just stuck here feeling uneasy?

"So?" Lotte scrutinized her expectantly.

The three of them froze, Jervey openmouthed, Fred blank,

and Lotte waiting. "I appreciate your asking me here," mumbled Jervey. "It was kind of you."

"We wanted to talk to you. We haven't had much chance at rehearsal." Lotte grinned, showing a mouthful of strong, square teeth. "You're a brave young girl to take on that play. It's not easy, is it? But you do well. You're shrewd, like Hap. Oh, your father! Now there was a special man, a genius. He led us all farther than we dreamed we could go. Such craft! Such enthusiasm! Do you remember that first production of the play?"

"Not well. I was about fifteen. I remember it was a hit."

"It was exceptional. And it will be this time." She patted Jervey's knee. "The young man, Chance—you're bringing him around, teaching him, leading him. Of course, he will be different from Keith."

"I barely remember Keith."

"A born actor." Lotte looked at Fred for confirmation.

"He was that," admitted Fred.

"His ability to make an audience laugh or cry," Lotte continued, "his generosity to other actors."

"He was sure of himself," added Fred. "Never a wrong move."

"I remember one night," said Lotte, "when Thad went blank, it happens to all of us. Never to Thad before. He couldn't remember the line, skipped a whole page ahead. Keith improvised, without missing a beat, got Thad back on track. The audience never knew, only the cast. Later, at the brush-up rehearsal, I asked Hap, in front of all, if he wasn't proud of Keith. You know Hap. He looked around and said that's what we're expected to do for each other." She laughed, glanced at Fred.

"I've got to get home." Fred pulled himself to his feet. He put his mug on the coffee table. "I'm expecting a call."

"I'd better go, too." Jervey rose.

97

"Wait." Lotte didn't comment on the shortness of their visit. "I have something for you to take home."

Fred and Jervey waited in silence while she went to the kitchen and returned with one of her decorative bakery boxes. "Apple strudel," she announced, handing it to Jervey.

"Can I drop you off, Jervey?"

"Thank you, Fred."

It wasn't until she was almost home, sitting rigidly, the box on her knees, Fred silent beside her, that she read her own body language. She'd absorbed but not until that moment admitted what was both obvious and appalling. His passion for gossip was too strong for Stanley to resist. He'd told one or all of them everything.

She heard the music before she opened the door. Strauss. She found that the long hall table had been moved against a wall to make room for the two couples dancing. Milo and Emma, Roberta and Chance Crown. They greeted her with smiles, but didn't stop or even hesitate. As Emma and Milo swung past her, Emma called out, "I'm learning to waltz."

Jervey thought at once of the Parmalee tradition of holding parties after funerals, the command in Hap's will that a gathering be held after the service. She remembered it vividly, the crowd, the singing, all the food and drink, and what Hap insisted on, "a celebration of life."

The romantic music with the improbable pairing of these dancers made her laugh. She saluted them, blew them a kiss, and went into the library. She sat, closed her eyes, and listened to the music. She didn't wonder why Chance was there. Roberta had seen him at the funeral, talked to him, and, as night follows day, invited him to the house. She tried to empty her mind, disengage herself. After a few minutes she could feel a slight but encouraging lift of the heart, a clarity of thought. By the time they joined her, she was prepared.

Roberta and Milo had a drink, Emma a Coke, and, in

deference to the Players rule about no booze before rehearsals or performances, Jervey and Chance drank coffee.

There was no talk of the funeral or the play. No one asked her where she had been. Roberta and Milo, prompted by the waltz, discussed the poor training American actors received compared to the British.

"A young actor here might be great in a Miller or Williams play," Milo observed, "but put him in Shakespeare or even Oscar Wilde and he's lost. He has no understanding of style. And there isn't time to teach it in rehearsal."

"Hap spent every summer teaching," said Roberta. "We had free classes at the playhouse four nights a week. He dealt a lot with style, the way the voice and the body can be used to reflect the period of a play. Nowadays . . ."

Jervey noticed that though Chance, in his beautifully tailored suit, was listening with interest, his glance kept returning to her. She couldn't read the look. She'd been wondering again and again what there was about Chance that worried Thad. It was hard to believe that he had a murky past, that he'd committed something illegal or immoral. But Thad wouldn't have warned her unless he really was concerned.

"Where have you been, Jervey?" Emma sat on the floor, her cards spread in a game of solitaire, her new blue skirt fanned out around her.

Jervey realized that the little face, framed by the cap of red curls, actually looked pretty. Emma's eyes, wide-set under delicately arched brows, reflected much more than a precocious intelligence.

"Lotte asked Fred and me to her house for a drink." She turned to Roberta. "And I'm pretty sure that Stanley told them about the bones, the whole story. Ma, I don't know why, but when I had a drink with him I told him everything, mainly to get a reaction, find out more about the cast. You know how he loves to talk."

99

"Oh Lord!" Roberta sighed. "You think they all know?"

"That I suspect there's a murderer in the cast? By now, yes."

"What will that do to the play?" asked Chance.

"Nothing." Milo reached for his pipe. "The innocent will apply themselves more diligently; the guilty, I should think, will try to appear most innocent."

"Milo, this play opens in a very short time. I have to go through rehearsals as if nothing's wrong. How can I—"

"The show," said Roberta grimly, "must go on."

"Guess what, Jervey?" Emma's face looked lit from within. "Chance is going to take me out in his boat tomorrow."

T e n

· · · · · ·

"Chance came by for Emma at the crack of dawn." Roberta, hair on end and wearing Hap's pajamas, sipped coffee and stared through the kitchen window. "She was beside herself with excitement. Why, I can't imagine. Paddling through swamps and swatting mosquitoes."

"I hope she took a sweater."

"She did, at my insistence. Also asked to borrow my double-drop pearl earrings."

"Did you agree?"

"Yes, out of gratitude."

"Gratitude?"

"That she's not mine."

"Ma!"

"Emma's quite smitten with Chance Crown."

"Is that why she cut her hair?"

"She cut her hair because she wants to look like you."

Taking a cup of coffee with her, Jervey went back to her room and crawled into bed with her script. Once again, she studied the symbols Hap had drawn beside each name. She asked herself the question Emma had asked, whether the symbols were Hap's key to the part being played by each person or to the person who was playing it.

Stanley, two profiles, back to back, two-faced, an Iago or a Gemini; Thad, a crown, symbol of authority, nobility; Fred, an eel, slippery, evasive; Elissa, an egg. Symbol of new life? No. Something to be handled carefully. Lotte, a rectangle or maybe, yes, a loaf of bread. Earth mother, quintessential cook. The dagger beside Keith's name was the most puzzling. It was obvious Keith was not popular. Stanley had no use for him and reported that Keith and Fred had come to blows. She was sure Lotte and Fred were lying in their praise of him. But a dagger, dangerous, lethal, had nothing to do with the part Keith played, the gentle son, Tim.

Did the dagger mean that Keith was a dangerous person or that his presence posed some threat to the cast? Or a threat to the balance of the play, a bone of contention? Knowing the way Hap's mind worked, she opted for the threat to the play. The show came first. Anything that created problems among cast members could damage the play. But the peril to the play should have been Elissa, Stanley's obsession, Thad's girlfriend, Fred's dream girl; Elissa dancing with Keith like Rogers and Astaire.

Rehearsal the night before had been smooth as silk. Most of them already knew all their lines. Chance was carefully slipping into the part of Tim, the look of a creature barely surviving in a hostile environment, his voice lighter, speech hesitant. When the energy level of the cast ebbed, it was Fred who picked it up, making points with greater clarity. Abby, playing the female counterpart of Tim, was giving the daughter's self-denial a strange but effective note of suspense. Lotte, Fred, all of them were immersed in their parts, a totality rare in a cast. Jervey was reminded of a New York friend, another

102

aspiring actress, who remarked, "I guess I love it because it's an escape, an alternate life. I can disappear into a part."

Jervey lay back on her pillow and thought about her cast. Considering it only as a mental exercise, she tried to picture each of them as a possible murderer. What could drive solid Thad to an act of violence? Rejected love? Maybe, but the love would have to be violent itself, all consuming. Thad was too balanced for that kind of passion. Lotte could be loving, even ardent, but rejection wouldn't move her to murder. Betrayal, perhaps. Stanley was hard to figure, Stanley with his Cadillac and the breakfast table set the night before, showering the unattainable Elissa with gifts, insisting she wasn't committed to any man. Abby, the stage manager without a symbol, the ugly duckling perhaps enamored of the charming Keith, having secret meetings with him, giving her all and then finding out she was a momentary diversion? Fred? In his inept way he'd made a play for Elissa, who'd been kind to him. Did he misread the kindness as a sexual response, think he was getting the gorgeous upper-class girl of his dreams, and then have Keith move in . . .

Maybe, maybe, maybe. Maybe the damn bones weren't Keith's at all. Maybe Keith was in Tampa or Birmingham or Altoona, playing parts, charming the ladies, and planning to move on. Plenty of people broke arms and legs. Maybe the whole contrived conjecture was a diversion for Roberta, Milo, Emma, and even herself. They had jumped to conclusions. They lived in a troubled world, depicted nightly on TV with treason, greed, jealousy, violence, and murder dramatized to entertain. They were programmed to be suspicious, to assume the worst. She found it impossible to suspect anyone in her cast. She was sick of the whole thing. It was time to put it behind her, get on with the play.

She stared at the ceiling. Things were going well. Tom Crain had finished the set, found someone to handle props. A veteran backstage worker had offered to stage-manage. The newsletter had been mailed to members and the programs were being printed. Posters were displayed in shops around town and in the mall. Yes, if she was to reveal a murderer it would have to be after the closing night of the play.

She thought of the group waltzing in the hall and grinned. She wondered what it would be like to waltz with Chance Crown. She discarded the thought. She concentrated on the play, hoping there were no crucial points she had missed. The music below had long ago ended, but she still was hearing it.

She told herself it was a rebound reaction to her fling with the brilliant Jason. She'd had one affair for two wrong reasons: (A) to prove that she wasn't frigid, as several scorned men suggested, and (B) to prove that she was part of the challenging end of the twentieth century.

Because of the way he looked, the life he led, she'd begun to enfable Chance Crown, endow him with all the old-fashioned manly virtues that she knew existed only between the covers of a book. The pre–New York Jervey would have been a victim of what she wanted to believe. The post–New York Jervey had had her eyes jerked open to some daunting home truths about men.

Even if Thad was wrong and Chance was just what he seemed, a relationship with him was out of the question. She envisioned a brief fling, passion among the pines, or crazier still a little family in that two-room hut, living on collard greens, insisting that they were right in abandoning the false values of a corrupt society.

Pleased by her cool-headed wisdom, she rewarded herself, lapsed into an indulgent reverie. She reviewed the open honesty in his blue eyes, the high cheekbones, his spare, muscular body, long sun-browned hands. She thought of the way he moved with balanced strides, the total lack of self-consciousness, his unawareness of the power of his presence.

She had to drag herself from this reverie, mentally put her head under a cold faucet. Either he was a fraud or Thad was wrong. Whatever he was, he wasn't for her. She might not end up as an actress or anyone of importance, but she would end up a realist, use whatever talents she possessed and not flounder through life with unreasonable expectations.

Roberta, wearing a fawn-tweed suit, alligator pumps, and a pleased smile, appeared in the doorway. "Milo and I are driving to Charleston to have lunch with the Pointers. Oh, and Abby and Thad have invited us to the Saturday night dinner dance at the country club." She laughed. "Undoubtedly they saw Milo with us in church and then at the funeral and are eaten with curiosity."

"Oh, Ma, not the country club!"

"I asked if we could bring Chance." At Jervey's reaction, Roberta softened her tone. "Sweetie, you don't want to drag through the whole evening dancing with old men."

Jervey spent the day alone. She went over her script. She wandered from room to room looking at the framed posters of Parmalee forebears in various parts. She paged through scrapbooks of news clippings, announcements of openings, faded reviews. She thought of the original Pa and Ma Parmalee touring all those southern towns for so many years, of Orlando, a generation later, rushing home from selling men's clothing at Drehers to eat a quick dinner and then hurry to the theater. And Hap. Hap and a few volunteers building scenery, creating Shangri-La or an English drawing room or a Brooklyn bar. Hap measuring actors for costumes and then making them himself, always with vision and vitality.

"Play the situation, work on each other for a response. The vitality must be there even in a quiet scene, an undercurrent of energy."

"What is your relationship with each other at the begin-

105

ning of the interval? What at the end? Where are the thrill moments, the frissons?"

The very air in the hushed old house seemed still charged with his drive and enthusiasm.

"Dad?" She looked slowly around the room.

Roberta and Milo returned late in the afternoon. Roberta announced that she planned to loll in a scented tub for an unspecified time and then take a nap. Milo went directly to the kitchen, removed his coat and tie, put on an apron, and proceeded to work on a *vitello tonnato* for the next day's supper. Jervey sat at the kitchen table and watched him take the veal from the fridge, make slits in it with a sharp knife, and put it in a heavy pot with a carrot, onion, lemon peel, and white wine.

She could see why Roberta found him a good companion. He approached everything with enthusiasm and style. His face, a classic English face, held an underlying merriment. Surely he was warmly welcomed in all the households where he chose to sponge, an improvident but charming addition.

Though she was determined to put the bones and Sully's death out of her mind, she found herself telling Milo about the symbols Hap had drawn by each name in his cast.

"What could an egg signify?" she asked him.

At first she thought he wasn't listening. He put a lid on the veal, adjusted the heat. "Fertility. Or maybe, fragility, someone to be handled with care." Jervey thought of Elissa, who'd had a breakdown, become an alcoholic, a recluse.

Milo took apples from a bag and began to core them. "Since we're talking about a cast, I'd say the fragility must be in relation to the other members. There must have been some threat to that breakability."

"The three men in the cast, four, counting Keith, were all enamored of her. But Elissa wasn't murdered."

"What about the other woman?"

106

"Lotte? Dad saw her as a loaf of bread, earth mother, I guess. Abby wasn't in the cast then."

"Earth mothers can be powerful. And nothing is more dangerous than power."

"Stanley's sign is a kind of double mask, back to back, a Janus. Two-faced?"

"Or unpredictable. In essence, two personalities."

Jervey wondered which one drove the Cadillac.

A loud clacking sound made them both jump. Jervey wheeled around, Milo dropped an apple. Emma stood in the doorway, double-drop earrings flashing. She made another strange clack, then grinned with delight. "The sound of the clapper rail or marsh hen," she proclaimed.

"Indeed," said Jervey weakly.

"We saw a whole bunch of them, and black-and-white oystercatchers and skimmers and grebes. Did you know that the marsh floods and then dries? It depends on the tide. When it drains you see a lot of little fiddler crabs going in and out of their holes. You see the tracks of herons and curlews and . . ." She sat at the table, drew a deep breath, pulled off the earrings. Milo exchanged a glance with Jervey and then reached for some raisins soaking in wine.

Jervey touched Emma's curly head. "I'm glad you had a good time."

Emma pulled a small notebook and a pencil from the pocket of her jeans. "Chance gave me these. He said it's fun to keep a list of all the birds you see. He's seen all of them. I wrote down most of what we saw today, but I've got to add a few." Clutching the pencil she bent over the notebook.

"What were the other symbols, Jervey?" Milo was filling the cored apples with wine-soaked raisins.

"An eel or a snake for Fred."

"Slippery comes to mind, of course. But considering your father's subtlety, I'd say that's too trite. An eel is seen by many

107

as a form of snake when, actually, it's a fish. Seen as one thing and, in truth, is another."

"The green-winged teal," murmured Emma as she wrote. "And the long-billed marsh hen."

"So you have two enigmas, the double-person Stanley and the deceptive Fred."

"Thad's sign is a crown."

"I'm going to put down the silver-winged fritillary. It's not a bird, it's a butterfly, because Chance said it reminded him of me." She gazed toward the window. "It's a beautiful orange-brown color."

"The crown," mused Milo, putting the apples in a baking dish. "Nobility."

"A ruler."

"Cormorants, grebes, wood storks."

"Yes," said Milo, "and as with Lotte's symbol, the sometime suggestion of power, tyranny."

"Everything depends on everything else in the marsh." Emma closed her notebook. "The birds, the fish, the crabs, the littlest forms of life. They're all connected." She regarded them solemnly. "It's a fragile ecology."

That night they rehearsed with all the props and, at the coffee break, discussed costumes. Since the play was set in the present, there were no problems as to what the men would wear. Thad and Stanley had suitable clothes. Chance, as Tim, would dress casually. Fred, playing the aging hippie, had the perfect wardrobe. Lotte had searched the costume room and found two dark print dresses, donated some years before, that were appropriately noncommittal. That left Abby.

"I have this gold wool dress," said Abby, "with a wonderful woven belt and a huge, marvelous buckle, or a turquoise knit, or—"

"You can't look smart or chic, Abby. Remember the girl you're playing wants to fade into the woodwork."

"But it's a rich family," Abby insisted. "She certainly would have nice clothes."

"Expensive, maybe," said Jervey, "but understated, unobtrusive. What did Elissa wear when she played the part?" She turned to Lotte.

Lotte stared at her, then laughed, a halfhearted honk. "Her own things. God knows she had enough, brought a whole suitcase—" She cut herself off, shrugged, went to refill her coffee cup.

Thad turned to Abby. "Why don't you just bring some dresses tomorrow night and let Jervey decide."

At the end of rehearsal she waited for Chance to shed his tights and ballet slippers and leave the theater before she could lock the doors. By the time he reappeared, everyone else had gone.

"Chance, I want to thank you for the good time you gave Emma."

"She's a really bright kid. I enjoyed it."

Jervey started down the aisle. "You opened a whole world for her. Her only contact with nature has been Central Park."

"I'd be glad to open that world for you."

"Thank you."

"When?" He stopped her in her tracks. She hesitated, unsure of how to answer.

"How about a week from today?"

"Good. I'll pick you up a week from today around five A.M."

Before she could comment on this, he took her arm, leading her down the aisle. "You know, that was a peculiar reaction tonight when Lotte mentioned Elissa's clothes."

"How do you mean?"

109

"Well, Lotte looked like she'd made a terrible mistake, told a lie or betrayed a confidence or something like that."

"What about the others?"

"They had the same look."

Eleven

She thought of the morning she'd ridden in this same truck after seeing Sully lying dead on the sidewalk. It seemed to have happened a long time ago. Time had both flown and dragged. But the play was shaping up, no crises. It had been a placid week. It had occurred to her only once that they all were walking on eggs.

She dozed as they drove in darkness for over an hour, finally jolted awake when they turned into a deeply rutted road. She had no idea where they were. She didn't know why she'd agreed to come. Her feelings about the man beside her were ambivalent to say the least. She assured herself that this brief excursion would help her to understand Emma's new enthusiasm, give them something to share.

Chance had spoken little since he knocked on her door before dawn. He didn't speak when he finally stopped the truck or when he took her arm as she stepped to the ground. He lifted the canoe from the back of the truck and carried it to a small dock, put a canvas carryall under one of the seats.

Sitting in the canoe, she barely was aware of movement as they glided forward in the semi-darkness. She was conscious of the slowly receding night, an encompassing silence. She saw that they were going through narrow spaces, flanked on either side by tall grass. At first she glimpsed only shadows, then dim forms, and then, after some minutes, a lightening on the horizon. The blackness of the sky had become purple, melting downward into a gray lilac. On what seemed the edge of the world, the sun began to rise, a brilliant orange-yellow. She heard one tinkling bell-like sound, followed by another and then another.

"Marsh wrens," whispered Chance.

To her left, in the far distance, she could find the shapes of trees. Just ahead of the canoe, something long and ridged slithered through the water.

"Alligator."

He looked toward the two tall, elegantly curved heads rising above the grasses. "Egrets."

It's like the beginning of the world, she thought. Each day must be like the beginning of the world. She drew in a deep breath of salt air, mingled with the smell of the marsh, earthy, fecund.

Eventually, they moved out into a wider body of water. The water itself was changing color, reflecting rose and orange, streaked with silver. The marsh had turned gold. From all around she began to hear bird voices, shrill, soft, piping, deep, celebrating the day.

Chance stopped paddling. They drifted. When he spoke, it was quietly, as if he were revealing a secret. "Jervey, everything here is interdependent. About every six hours the tide floods, covering the marsh grass, bringing in what the shellfish need to live. It also brings in fish and other creatures who feed and mate. Then, when the tide recedes, you have shore birds, raccoons, and others who come to forage in the mud flats. If

112

you close your eyes, you can feel the energy here, life-forms dependent on other life-forms, a cycle that never stops.

"The next time we come I'll show you the swamp forests. You'll have a real sense of wilderness. Black water, reflections of cypress draped with moss. Up in Four Hole Swamp there's the world's last big tract of original-growth bald cypress and tupelo gum, some as old as six hundred years."

"This is your workplace?"

"Yes. Conservation officers check hunters and fishermen to make sure they have permits, licenses, and safe equipment. Hunting is completely regulated, from the taking of certain species to bag limits, to the time and season of the hunt. Often I go after night hunters and people who drag for shrimp in illegal areas. I had to get another officer to cover for me while I'm being an actor.

"Right now," he said, "this whole area looks the way it might have when the Indians paddled through these waters, before the era of the rice plantations. When the rice culture died out, nature reclaimed its own."

Finally he turned the canoe, paused to look around him, then resumed paddling. "The swamp forests are where you'll find the wild turkeys, bobcats, deer, duck." There was a kind of reverence in his voice. It reminded her of the way Father Jake said prayers, with an underlying amazement.

"What you're seeing now is protected. Some of the land-owners, plantation people, are making sure that this can never be changed, developed. But there are other parts that still are endangered." He put up his paddle and they drifted. She watched fish jumping, birds rising out of the marsh grass.

He reminded her of someone else. Hap. Hap talking about theater, about preserving the ancient theatrical means of communication, what he called "the basics of the craft."

The water was reflecting the spreading blueness of the sky. The marsh grass rose in strokes of gold. Eyes wide, hands

113

grasping the sides of the canoe, she sat stiffly erect, trying to see it all, knowing that this first-time experience would stay with her forever.

After they'd docked and Chance had carried the canoe back to the truck, she tried to think of a way to thank him, to tell him what the morning had meant to her. She couldn't find the words.

Once more they rode in a comfortable silence. It wasn't until they turned into the driveway of her house that she finally spoke. "Chance, if I ask you a question, will you give me a straight answer?"

"Sure."

"Promise?"

"Promise." He stopped the car at the veranda steps, turned to look at her, his eyes serious.

"Why did you agree to be in the play?"

He looked into her eyes for a long moment, started to say something, stopped. When he did speak, there was a gravity in his voice as well as in his eyes. "I'd rather wait before I answer that. It's a bigger question than you think."

"It is?"

"And I've not found the words to answer it." He grinned suddenly. "I'm not a word man."

"I've noticed."

She did not invite him in for breakfast or attempt to thank him. He wasn't a word man.

Roberta, Milo, and Emma looked up as she entered the kitchen, their faces bright, expectant. She ignored the communal bated breath and poured herself a cup of coffee.

"Well?" Roberta could wait no longer.

"Well what?"

"Are you going to become a Girl Scout? Are you heading for Outward Bound?"

"I'm heading for a quick nap."

"Did you see an alligator?" asked Emma. "Or an egret or a cormorant?"

"I saw everything."

They watched her as she carried her cup across the room, left the kitchen, and headed upstairs. Emma followed, talking without pause. "I'd like to see a real skink and hide in the dunes some night and watch those big turtles come out of the ocean and lay their eggs. Did you know that as soon as the baby turtles hatch, they head for the water? How old do you think Chance is? It's hard to raise a deer in captivity and then expect it to adapt to the wild. Don't you think he looks a little like Nick Nolte? If I had to be a bird, I think I'd be an eagle. Eagles are the most powerful. Even animals respect them. They're so fierce, so beautiful . . ."

Emma followed her into her room, but she turned the child around, patted her head, shoved her gently back into the hall, and closed the door.

She didn't take a nap. She sat on the window seat, holding but not drinking the cup of coffee, and looked down at the overgrown shrubs, trees beginning to turn color. A bird perched on a branch by the window stared at her.

She never had been one for scrupulous self-examination. Trying to analyze behavior, yes, because it was part of theater. But she wasn't given to dissecting her life, evaluating every relationship in a never-ending quest for "self-realization." She knew that when she was twelve she wanted to be part of the gang. She was and she wasn't. She learned to accept and then protect her differentness. When she was sixteen she wanted to be part of a couple. She was and she wasn't. She had dates, went to school dances, but declined to be clumsily pawed in parked cars. During the college years she seemed to date men who were brainy, offbeat, and, in one way or another, misfits. Misfits, the too brilliant, the emotionally

115

lame, halt, and blind, were drawn to her. She'd been drawn to Jason because he appeared a man in control, leaning on no one. She'd met him when her self-esteem was at low ebb. Desperately lonely and unsure of her abilities as an actress, as well as a woman, she was stunned to find that she'd attracted a man as brilliant as Jason. Or as worldly and witty, the creator, he admitted, of dark, dazzling elliptical poems. With consummate skill, he'd lured her into an affair that was to her the ultimate romance and to him a capricious if amusing fling with an improbable naïf.

She had grown up in Hap's world of the theater, make-believe. As a child, seeing her first play, a production of *Sleeping Beauty,* she'd known that the actors were pretending; she'd been backstage, seen them putting on makeup, getting into costume. She knew it was man-made magic. Yet she was pulled at once into the fable, entranced, translating it into a private reality. If she had a fatal weakness, it was that she fell victim to dreams, reached defiantly for the mirage. Only if she was vigilant would it be less than fatal.

That afternoon Roberta announced that she was going to the beauty parlor. Jervey, sitting in the bathtub, looked up at her in surprise. "Why? The dance isn't until Saturday night."

Roberta perched on the edge of the tub, her face set in lines of pleasure and determination. "I like to check out the opera-tors. Alma Branch Crosland told me that Sharon Fleet works at the Hair Flair Salon. She's supposed to be a wizard. Alma Branch also dropped the fact that Sharon started out, years ago, as a maid at the Dowells'. Elissa Dowell's family, Jervey. This was before Elissa had the breakdown."

"Oh, Ma!"

"A wash, a rinse, a cut, a mousse, and maybe some riveting info about the poor blighted Elissa."

"Good luck, Miss Marple."

Jervey and Emma spent the afternoon looking for a birth-

116

day present for Emma's mother. At first, Emma, having no money, halfheartedly suggested making her a gift, a drawing or a pot holder. When she agreed to accept a loan, they headed for the mall.

Jervey was continually surprised by Emma's devotion to a mother who alternately spoiled, neglected, and totally ignored her. In the past weeks there had been no calls from Deirdre, not so much as a postcard. Yet Emma had realistically settled for what Deirdre had to offer. Or had she? Watching Emma's face, pink with excitement as they went from shop to shop looking for the perfect gift, Jervey realized how much Emma longed to please her mother. Out of that pleasure might come a moment of complete attention, even affirmation.

They considered costume jewelry, scarves, T-shirts. In a bookstore, Emma leafed through volumes on various methods of self-discovery. They sat on a bench by the mall's fountain and discussed sending cut flowers or a plant. It wasn't until they were leaving that Emma, passing a bizarre little shop, found her heart's desire. It was a small cloth and china harlequin, a spindly clown figure with a mysterious smile.

"That's it!"

"A doll?"

"She'll love it! I know she'll love it!"

Once they were back in the car, heading home, Emma unwrapped the doll, examined it carefully. "She can hang it in a window, maybe. No, it can sit on the mantel."

When they arrived at the house, they found Roberta and Milo in the library. Roberta, holding a notebook and pencil, sat on the sofa. Her hair was styled in what looked like a stainless steel pageboy. Milo sat at the long table behind the sofa, surrounded by papers. Wearing his glasses and an air of benign consternation, he looked like a clip from *Goodbye, Mr. Chips*.

"Look what we found!" Emma raced to Roberta, held up the harlequin.

"Marvelous!" Roberta touched the mysterious little masked face. "I want one just like it."

"My mother collected harlequins," said Milo, removing his glasses, "but that's a particularly beguiling one."

"It's for my mother's birthday."

"She'll be delighted," Milo assured her.

Jervey stared at the papers in front of Milo. "What are you doing, Milo? Writing your memoirs?"

"It's my bookkeeping." Roberta regarded the papers with disgust. "He hopes to keep me out of jail for unpaid taxes and insurance fraud."

"Ma, your hair's a fright."

"It's worth it." She held up her notebook. "Sharon isn't an inspired beautician but she's an absolute treasure trove of information. Of course, it took a while. During the wash and rinse I was forced to listen to her rather murky view of life, the stupidity of women, the self-serving bestiality of men. While she assaulted, tormented, moussed, and sculpted my hair, I heard all about the merciless behavior of the upper class toward household employees."

"Did she really work for the Dowells, Ma?"

"Not only that. She was unjustly fired for theft. Accused and then released because of insufficient evidence."

"Theft of what?"

"Elissa's jewelry."

Nobody spoke, so Roberta continued. "A week or so after Elissa's suicide attempt and departure to the clinic, it was discovered that her jewelry was gone, as well as a lot of clothes. The other servants had worked there for years. Sharon was the newcomer and therefore suspect."

Jervey sank into a chair. "What's Sharon's view of all this?"

Roberta slipped neatly into a Piedmont accent. "I knowed

118

right away what happened. I seen her all them times, him an' her, dancin' from room to room when her folks was off somewheres. I seen the way she looked at him. They was fixin' to take off, you better believe it. I even seen her goin' down the back steps with her bags that day, then puttin' them in the trunk of her fancy car."

Roberta stopped, looked at each of their faces. "When I asked her what day that was, she said, 'Hell, I don't carry no calendar around in my head.' "

"Did the police believe all this?"

"Of course not. They found no suitcases in Elissa's car. Elissa by this time was incommunicado, staring into space. But Sharon was sprung from jail almost at once."

"How come, Ma?"

"The Dowells very suddenly dropped charges."

"Wow!" whispered Emma.

"What have we got so far?" asked Milo.

Roberta consulted her notebook. "We have the bones with the fractured leg, the hearing aid, and now Sharon's saga. We have four men in the cast, all besotted with Elissa. We have Elissa, on some date, packing her things, supposedly for departure."

"But she didn't depart," said Emma. "Keith did." Her eyes sparkled. "Maybe he swiped her things and then took off."

"Quite possibly," said Roberta, "what Elissa thought. From what I remember the lady was none too stable. Beautiful, cosseted, but emotionally fragile. If she was all that wild about Keith, planning to elope with him—"

"And let's say," Milo picked it up, "that she went to the theater on the closing night of the play and she and Keith transferred her bags to his car, intending for them to go to the cast party later and then, at an opportune moment, leave. Did she drive to the party alone, Roberta?"

"As I remember, she did. She came early, tried to help me with the food."

"Did she stay long?"

"Yes. I think she did. Yes! She was one of the last to leave."

"Where were her other admirers, Ma—Thad, Stanley, Fred? I mean at the end of the party?"

"They'd gone."

"Did Keith stay at the party, Ma? Think! Was he one of the last to leave?"

Roberta paused, stared at Jervey. "You know, I can't remember. I can't remember even seeing him."

"He was lying dead in that mummy case," said Emma grimly.

"Ma, are you sure all the other men in the cast showed up at the party?"

"As far as I know. Fred was a little late—I remember that. Said he had to stop somewhere and pick up his date. Undoubtedly, he hoped to make Elissa jealous. As it turned out, his date changed her mind."

"You can remember all that?" asked Emma, impressed. "After ten years?"

"It was an unforgettable night, with the fire and all. Etched on my brain."

"I think Abby is the murderer." Emma inspected the harlequin. "She'd had an affair with Keith and then she found out about him and Elissa. In a fit of passionate rage, she slew him in the shower."

"If there was a murder," said Jervey reluctantly, "then the guilty person was the one who pushed Sully from that window. Sully, in all innocence, may have known something, or it was believed that he did." She smiled at Emma. "I don't think Abby slew Keith, because, at the time of Sully's death, she was driving around looking for Thad to give him a message from someone at Accrolux."

120

"Thad and Lotte were walking or jogging together, at some point," mentioned Roberta. "What about Stanley and Fred?"

Nobody answered. Milo put his glasses in his pocket, rose. "I shall leave you to your conjectures and go check the beef bourguignon."

"I have this friend," Emma announced, "whose aunt is a Cordon Bleu cook. She studied in Paris."

Twelve

Saturday came too quickly. Jervey had been avoiding all thought of the country club dance, torn between dread and ridiculous, sneaking spasms of anticipation. She reminded herself again that the play would be opening in another week and she and Emma would head for New York. She had been able to generate a certain cynicism in regard to Chance Crown. She considered knowing him as a learning experience. She had learned that she must be vigilant in spotting her vulnerable reactions to certain men. Besides, Thad never would have alluded to something unfortunate in Chance's background without some certainty.

She stared at the dress spread out on her bed. When she'd tried to avoid the dance by announcing she had nothing to wear, her mother had hotfooted it to the theater and returned with costumes for both of them, Hap's creations.

"I," said Roberta, "shall wear this." She'd held up a cerise satin, bias-cut evening dress, slit to the hip and with rhinestone shoulder straps. "Remember? I wore this for the tango number in *Ring Round the Moon.*"

"This is for you." She'd handed Jervey a diaphanous chiffon creation, strapless, with a tight-fitting bodice. The eight yards of material flowed from leaf green to deep emerald.

"Cynthia Parker wore it in *The Philadelphia Story*. It's your size. The color's perfect for you."

"I have a friend," Emma had remarked, "who's just my age and she's already been to four dances. Her mother wants her to learn social grace."

"We've engaged a sitter," said Roberta firmly, "and the larder will be stocked with Coke, pizzas, chips, and frozen Snickers bars."

"I haven't had a sitter since I was six years old. Sitters are always airheads."

"This one's a Ph.D."

Reluctantly dressing for the big evening, Jervey had negative thoughts about the country club. In the old days it was rather charmingly low-key, an antebellum-type edifice, always in need of repair, offering a bar, a dining room, and a good-sized area for dancing and receptions. Behind the building there were two tennis courts. All the members knew each other. They went to the club for debuts, wedding parties, bridge tournaments, and fund rallies. The annual fees barely kept the place afloat. The food was passable, except for the fried chicken, which was A-1.

The current club, taken over by the Accrolux group, had been enlarged, on all sides, to include men's and women's gyms with saunas, a much larger cypress-paneled bar, and a chandeliered reception room the size of a baseball field. Golfers came from all over to play the Oldport championship course.

While she showered and applied a modicum of makeup, Jervey thought about being fourteen and going to her first dance, a high school prom, held at the country club because the school gym was under repair. Her date for the evening was Bro Closters, who was as tall, skinny, and as socially insecure as she. His invitation was offhand, to say the least.

"You going to the dance?"

"No."

"My mother's been leaning on me to go. Yuk."

"I know what you mean."

"Listen, we could go and then leave early."

"Yeah."

Despite the uninspired exchange, Jervey had dressed with dreamy anticipation in a gown Hap had made for the occasion, white silk, trimmed with little seed pearls. She remembered that the bodice was minutely pleated and tucked to make her look like she actually possessed a bosom.

Bro called for her half an hour late. While Hap and Roberta watched with pride and sickeningly sentimental grins, he'd presented her with a dispirited carnation corsage and whisked her away in his daddy's car.

She'd noticed that his eyes were glazed and his driving erratic, but she stared straight ahead, envisioned herself dancing with someone like Thad Egan.

Not only was her dress too fancy, provoking amused stares from the other girls, but Bro, after a few steps on the crowded dance floor, turned an odd shade of green and threw up all over the too-fancy dress and himself.

Ready at last, she coldly surveyed herself in the mirror. She had to admit that the dress was flattering. She twirled around, watching the way the skirt rose, drifted out, and then fell. She realized, with a cynical amusement, that the girl in the mirror was the incarnation of the dreamy self-destructive part of her that she'd finally cast into outer darkness. She smiled at herself, touched the cap of shiny, dark curls, noted the soft oval face, long graceful neck, smooth young shoulders. Why not play it the way she looked? Have a ball? What the hell. She went downstairs.

The two men stood by the library fireplace. She'd expected Milo to look devastating in evening clothes and he did. Chance was barely recognizable. He'd had a haircut and the thick mane was neatly combed except for one streaked lock that hung over his forehead. His dinner jacket and trousers fit perfectly. His tucked white shirt was dazzling, black tie impeccable. He wore neither muddy boots nor moccasins nor ballet slippers, but like Milo black patent leather evening shoes.

Milo and Chance stared at her for several seconds and then Milo let out a low dignified whistle. "Jervey, don't move. I want to remember you this way always."

"From an old play or a film, Milo?"

"I think it was a film. George Brent and Irene Dunne."

She joined them. Milo plucked the champagne bottle from the cooler and poured her a glass. Chance turned and examined the poster of Pa Parmalee over the mantel. Jervey marked that he'd barely looked at her.

"Are you ready for this?" Roberta struck a pose in the doorway. It was outrageous for a woman her age to be wearing a skin-tight satin dress, slit on one side to the hip, to be baring arms, shoulders, and neck no longer young. She'd added a rhinestone choker and brushed her hair into a French twist, adorned with a curved black feather.

My Lord, thought Jervey, she'll get away with it.

"Rhinestones are a girl's best friend," breathed Milo.

Emma joined them and was allotted one glass of champagne. She studied each of them, her eyes wide. Roberta plucked at one of the red curls. "Emma," she said drily, "don't you have a friend whose mother went to a dance at the Grand Trianon?"

125

"No." Emma met her glance. "It was Buckingham Palace."

The sitter wasn't a Ph.D., just a lowly M.A. A dark, spindly girl with an armful of books, she had a no-nonsense air. "We'll do just fine," she said, eyeing Emma. "I've had two courses in early childhood development."

"God help her," laughed Roberta as they climbed into Milo's car.

Why, wondered Jervey as they drove along the dusky streets, was getting ready for a party almost always better than the party itself? She was acutely aware of Chance sitting beside her on the backseat staring through the window. The closeness they'd shared the morning in the marsh must have been imagined. He looked not only urbane but remote. Only his darkly tanned hand, resting on one knee, seemed familiar.

Abby and Thad lived just beyond the town in what once had been a dense pine forest. It was now a stylish development of sizable estates. All the roads were smoothly paved and marked, each walled estate approached through impressive gates. Roberta, the only one who knew the way, directed Milo.

"I've not been in the house," she said, "but I predict an impeccable if sterile arrangement of Old Heritage reproductions and prints of Audubon prints."

The house, rising at the end of the drive, was derivative of what was called "Country Georgian"—clean, spare lines, an understated dignity. Huge oaks grew on either side and just beyond. A maid in a dark uniform and starched white apron opened the front door before they touched the knocker. She led them into a spacious hallway with polished floors and a huge bouquet of fall flowers on a central table. Jervey saw a formal drawing room on one side, with taupe walls and white woodwork. Opposite, she saw Pompeiian red walls, more white woodwork, walls of books.

"Roberta, Jervey, Chance!" Thad emerged from the library to welcome them. He acknowledged the introduction to Milo, led them into the room. Lotte and Stanley, like characters in a dressy comedy, sat on paisley sofas that faced each other on either side of the fireplace. Abby rose at once. She acknowledged Roberta and Jervey with a warm smile, surveyed the suave Chance with some surprise, and shook hands with Milo. She wore an elegant black faille evening suit, a narrow skirt with a fitted jacket. Her only adornment was earrings, diamond and turquoise.

"Abby, your house is a wonder." Roberta's voice was sincere.

"Thank you, Roberta." Abby's voice was impressively regal. "Would you and Jervey like to see the rest of it?"

"We'd love to," said Jervey. She was grateful that Abby seemed neither stunned nor appalled by Roberta's costume.

"Me, too." Lotte hoisted herself from the sofa and joined them. Jervey noticed that she'd bagged ethnicity for the evening and worn a brown silk skirt and an ivory satin jacket. The long braid was wound around her head.

As they moved from room to room, Jervey couldn't resist giving her mother a "you were wrong" look. Far from sterile, the house had undeniable charm. There were no Old Heritage reproductions. The Sheraton and Hepplewhite pieces in the drawing room were obviously authentic, as was the Duncan Phyfe dining table in the room beyond. She could almost hear Roberta mentally ticking off points: French silk in the drawing room; hand-blocked English linen in the dining room; English watercolors; Renoir and Matisse drawings, and Braque etchings.

The bedrooms were spacious and welcoming, not prettily pastel, but decorated in muted colors, emphasizing the big windows looking over garden and woods. The master bedroom was the largest, a proper setting for the canopied bed, chaise longue, matching antique chests of drawers. Above the mantel hung a portrait of Abby, the pattern of flowers in her filmy dress duplicating the basket of flowers she held in her lap. The artist saw her as triumphantly beautiful, either finding or imposing a look of sly elation.

"An amazing portrait," said Roberta softly.

Jervey knew that she and her mother shared the same thought, "a perceptive artist." She found herself feeling sorry for the once cowed, not too attractive woman who had brilliantly re-created herself. She hoped that Abby's marriage to Thad was worth it. Though he seemed content, Thad hardly could be described as a doting husband.

Having grown up amid a profusion of family photographs, old posters, relics, and mementoes, Jervey noticed the absence of these. It was as if Abby and Thad had been born the day they moved into the house.

Abby must have been reading her mind. "I've always hated clutter," she said. "I was raised in small rooms with heavy furniture and a mishmash of Victorian junk."

As they started to leave the room, Abby stopped them. "Roberta, Jervey, we've been talking—Lotte, Thad, Stanley, and I—about doing something for Sully."

"If you mean a gravestone, Abby," said Roberta, "we've already arranged for that."

"No, not a stone. Something to be hung in the theater, a small brass or bronze plaque, maybe. To commemorate all the years he worked there, his devotion."

Roberta said nothing. Jervey rushed to agree. "I think that's a great idea. Wouldn't he love that, Ma?"

"Poor old Sully." Lotte shook her head. "So grateful for anything." She laughed, an uneasy bark. "How he loved sweets."

"He certainly did," said Abby. "I took him some cookies just the afternoon before he died. He told me about the cake you brought him, Jervey, the one we had left over after rehearsal. Lotte, he kept the box. He thought it was beautiful."

Lotte's color was poor. She turned to leave the room. "We'll bring it up at the annual meeting, about the plaque."

As the six of them sat in the Pompeiian red library, having drinks, Jervey had a distinct feeling of unreality. It was so civilized, so clearly a moment of gracious living, the men talking about land development, the women chatting about interior decoration, clothes, exchanging bits of gossip. And one of us, she thought, might be, to put it bluntly, a murderer.

She wondered why Abby and Thad hadn't invited Fred. Perhaps they felt he was a social risk, a feed and grain store manager who'd have to rent a tux. No. She was being unfair. She looked at Thad and Abby. They were not snobs. They were a stunning couple who belonged in their charming home. Maybe they invited Fred and he declined. She thought of Roberta's saying that Fred came late to the party on the night of the play's closing, ten years ago, because his date stood him up. There was something pitiful about Fred.

"Roberta, you look fantastic," Lotte was saying. "Such flair, imagination."

"Yes," Abby agreed. "Wherever did you find such a dress?"

"Paris," lied Roberta smoothly, "years ago. But the good designers never go out of style." She turned to Jervey, who was staring into space. "Don't you agree, darling?"

"What? Sure. You bet, Ma." For some reason she was remembering Stanley's remark about seeing Lotte giving money to the mysterious Keith. What was the tie? Lotte having an affair with a needy lover? Blackmail?

Jervey stood up and moved to where the men were standing.

129

"Jervey!" Thad reached out and pulled her to his side. "I was telling Chance what a superb actress you are."

"She certainly is," said Stanley, his watery eyes bright. "We were talking about that part you played in *The Chalk Garden,* Jervey, the teenage girl. You were so—so—"

"Touching and believable." Thad kissed her gently on the cheek. "The Parmalee heritage." She couldn't help noticing the grim look on Stanley's face, his mouth a hard line.

"I think we'd better head for the club." Abby's voice was light but firm. "They stop serving dinner at eight."

They joined the festivities at the tag end of the cocktail hour. Several hundred people were milling about in the bar and reception room, a few already heading for the dining room. The decibel level was deafening. Jervey noticed a predominance of northeastern and midwestern accents. Thad introduced them to a confusing number of his friends, unperturbed by their joking comments.

"Can't wait to see that play, Thad. Do you get to kiss the girl?"

"Hear you got hidden talents, old boy. Why waste your time being a lawyer?"

Every so often a woman would make it through the crowd to stand at Thad's side. Each had the same look of devotion. Jervey couldn't make out what they were saying but occasionally heard Thad's reassuring remarks.

"Janice, just do what we talked about. Don't worry, dear."

"Marie, you're going to be fine. Would I lie to you?"

"Sarah, if you need me, don't hesitate to call. Promise?"

Happily, Abby seemed ignorant of these encounters. Her back to Thad, she was talking Junior League to a thin, tawny woman with a wristful of gold chains and two other stylish if severe-looking Accrolux wives.

"Did Beverly tell you the meeting is Wednesday instead of Thursday, Abby?"

"Abby, I hope you and Thad can come to brunch on Sunday. It'll be small, only about thirty."

The women's clothes were smart, understated, and expensive, Jervey noted. After a casual glance at her green chiffon, all eyes, male and female, were fixed on Roberta. The reactions ranged from amazement to a peculiar kind of awe. Followed by the gorgeous Milo, Roberta moved through the throng, nodding coolly. Tallulah Bankhead as Catherine the Great.

The dining room glowed. Each table was lit by candles and had a delicate centerpiece of gold and rust flowers. French doors opened to an enormous terrace of polished brick with tubs of topiary trees. A well-manicured lawn stretched toward the woods beyond.

The eight of them shared a table. During the *pâté de foie gras en brioche* they discussed the changes in Oldport, Thad and Abby pro, Roberta and Milo anti, Lotte and Stanley ambivalent. No one seemed to notice that neither Jervey nor Chance cast a vote. While they enjoyed an excellent roast filet of beef with cornichon-tarragon sauce and lemon bulgur timbales, the conversation, led by Abby, moved to the magnificent offerings of England, the castles, the charming hamlets, and, of course, the cultural cornucopia of London. Jervey realized that this was chiefly for Milo's benefit. Milo, complimented to be perceived as British, played it to the hilt, spoke of Sunday polo matches with Prince Charles and Prince Philip, referred to the queen as Betty Windsor.

The surprise came when Abby turned to Chance and apologized. "This must be boring to someone whose life is rooted in the Low Country."

"Not at all, Abby. I was remembering the first polo match I saw in India, trying to remember when. I know it was the same year I ran with the bulls at Pamplona."

Jervey listened openmouthed as Chance and Milo compared great hotels, great wines, and music festivals. They compared the art treasures of the Louvre, the Prado, the Pitti Palace, and the British Museum. Chance, like Milo, was articulate, urbane, and extremely knowledgeable.

Abby and Lotte listened to them, entranced. Stanley concentrated on his food, frowning. Thad was unreadable. Roberta, on the other hand, looked vastly amused.

"Milo, Chance," said Abby, almost humbly, "there's a painting at this gallery in Charleston that I'm thinking of buying, an eighteenth-century Dutch landscape. I wish one or both of you would come with me one day and give your opinion."

"Of course," said Chance.

"Delighted," said Milo.

Jervey glared at the *crème génoise* just placed before her. She felt stupid, the poorest judge of men in the whole Southeast. What she had perceived as a simple, wide-eyed outdoorsman was something quite alien, opposite. One hardly could credit a swamp rat growing up dirt poor and then meandering about the capitals of Europe only to return and become a conservation officer. Like Milo, he was playing a part. Hap was right. In one way or another, everyone played a part. The world was a stage. She, alone, appeared to be uncast. She must pick a part, play it to the hilt.

From the big reception room came the sounds of an orchestra. Jervey conjured her most winsome smile and it fell on Thad.

"Jervey, may I have the first dance?"

It was old-time slow dancing; as Thad held her close, she thought of her teenage dreams of dancing with him. She ignored the fact that the electric thrill was missing. She moved from one set of arms to another, dreaming, dimpling, and sparkling like the most mindless of southern belles. Young men, old men kept cutting in, the music getting faster, wilder.

She saw Chance dancing with Roberta, Abby, Lotte, and then a profusion of young women. She saw Stanley, standing in a doorway, a drink in his hand, looking above it all.

A roll of drums ended her dance with a rather lecherous young executive in a plaid cummerbund. She saw Milo walk away from the orchestra leader and join Roberta. The daring first chords of the tango were like a call to volunteers for a dawn raid against the enemy. Some people fled to their tables, others pressed against walls to observe. A brave few sidled forward and slid into hesitant steps. Then Roberta and Milo took the floor. They moved at first with contrived coolness, an artful subtlety. They were the essence of smoothness, seduction. All eyes followed them. Keen as whips, their bodies straightened, then curved, then melted together, then moved apart. They were Vernon and Irene, Ginger and Fred. When, at the finale, Milo dipped Roberta backward, her head touching the floor, there was a great communal gasp. It reminded Jervey of Chance leaping from the wings. She saw him at the other end of the room, a small blonde clinging to his arm.

The orchestra launched into a polka. A portly man and a younger type approached her. She ducked away, slipped through the crowd, hurried across the dining room, and found an open French door.

It was a soft, limpid night with a three-quarter moon. The terrace was empty. She drew in a deep breath, felt like an actress who'd finished a difficult scene and made it to the wings. She looked across the dark lawn to the woods beyond. She found herself wondering about all the hidden life there, the birds, animals, plants, and insects, and was amazed that she'd had such a thought.

She decided that Chance was making a point of not dancing with her. Quite possibly this world-traveled, backwoods loner didn't want to encourage her. He had danced with

Roberta, Abby, and Lotte. She cringed at the thought that he'd seen a look in her eyes that made him want to spare her disappointment. She wondered who he was dancing with now.

She shivered and, as she did, arms closed around her from behind. She didn't look, speak, or even breathe.

"The bell of the ball alone on the terrace?" he said softly. "Waiting for the pumpkin coach?"

"Oh, Thad." She took a gulp of air.

"Jervey, honey." He turned her around. Head on one side, he looked at her, his face not only handsome but somehow young in the moonlight. "Are you all right?"

"I'm fine, Thad." How many times he'd asked that in the past. It was the first thing he said to Roberta when he'd come by the house after Hap died. He'd said it to her at her farewell party before going to New York. She thought of all the women coming up to Thad that night and realized that, though they might be physically attracted to him, their big need was for simple attention, concern.

"I guess you'll be going back to New York after the show opens."

"Yes."

"Jervey, have you considered staying on here? You could be permanent director. You're certainly good enough."

"Thank you, Thad, but I—"

"I don't mean to interrupt." Stanley appeared out of no-where, both hesitant and insistent.

Thad spoke a bit curtly. "I was just checking to see if Jervey would like a drink. Would you, dear?"

"No. Thank you, Thad."

"Well, in that case, I'll return to the fray. Stanley, have you danced with all the debs and dowagers?"

"I'm not much of a dancer."

"Try a few steps with Jervey. She makes everyone look

134

good." He touched her arm and walked back through the lighted doorway.

Stanley inched closer to her, too close. "I heard what Thad said about your staying on as director. He's right. You could do it, Jervey. The theater's been going downhill since we lost Hap. Of course, it would be a sacrifice for you, giving up the big time."

She could think of no reply.

"I have some books in my car, Jervey. I've been going through my library, thinning it out, and I found a lot of books on theater, some of them technical, some biographies, anthologies. I think you should have them. Oh, and I found this." He fished something from his pocket, held it out to her. "It once belonged to Ellen Terry, you know, the great actress. I found it in an antique store in Savannah."

Jervey looked at the charming brooch, a flower, delicately defined in topaz and diamonds. She realized then, with a sinking feeling, that she was the newly selected object of Stanley's obsessive, if asexual devotion. She had a feeling that the pin had been bought for Elissa.

"Stanley, it's too beautiful and too expensive. I wouldn't feel right. It's very sweet of you, but—"

"No!" He reached out, started to pin the brooch to the neckline of her dress, fumbling, hands unsteady. "It's for you. It's just right for you, Jervey. Please!"

She couldn't see the deep-set eyes in the shifting moonlight. The sockets looked dark, empty. She thought of the narrow bleakness of his life, the fact that outside of his job and whatever home life he shared with his sister, the theater was all that he had. "Thank you, Stanley," she said gently. "Bless you."

"I was watching you dance, Jervey, and you're the prettiest woman here. That dress is perfect for you. It looks even better

135

than it did on Cynthia. I remember. I was in *The Philadelphia Story*."

He leaned in, even closer. "Have you found out any more about those bones in your attic? I've been thinking about it a lot and—"

"Stanley, did you tell anyone, anyone at all about it?"

He didn't answer at once. When he did, there was a hurt note in his voice. "You know I wouldn't do that, Jervey."

She decided to believe him. "I think I would like a drink, after all, Stanley. Would you get me a scotch and soda?"

"Of course, Jervey." With the air of Lancelot mounting his steed, he took off.

She drew several deep breaths. In a matter of days, she vowed to herself, I'll be out of all this. I'll be in my New York nest, waiting for a callback, going to auditions. She pictured herself and Emma in the tiny apartment. She had a gut feeling that Deirdre wasn't ready to reclaim her child. It would be up to her to figure out how to get Emma to and from school, to see that she had decent meals. She hoped that Emma's level-headed acceptance of her mother's neglect didn't mask an impending emotional crisis.

"Roberta says we should think about leaving."

No arms slipping around her from behind, no soft voice saying, "Shall we dance?"

She swung around and faced him. "Are you sure you're ready? Aren't there one or two women you haven't danced with yet?"

"Two. Ashley Parker broke the heel on her shoe and Miss Althea Munn has hip dysplasia."

"You shone like a star at dinner. I especially enjoyed hearing about the art treasures of Europe. A far cry from egrets and raccoons."

"Protective coloring. Or as you might say, playing the scene."

"I underestimated you. Up until tonight I'd seen only the tidied-up swamp rat with a little Baryshnikov thrown in. Is there more to learn?"

"Are you implying tragedy or disgrace, something that made a spoiled rich kid abandon the fleshpots and disappear into the marsh?"

"You're under no obligation to be honest with me."

"There are a lot of things I don't know about you."

"True."

He walked to the low terrace wall, looked toward the distant woods. "We'll have rain before morning."

"Are you having a good time?"

He shrugged. "It's educational. As you know, I'm an observer of wildlife, survival patterns. Incidentally, you play the scene pretty well yourself. You must have danced with every man here."

"All except the second vice-president of sales. He passed out in the men's room."

"You haven't danced with me."

"You haven't asked."

He rubbed his chin, looked down at her. "The setting is wrong. I'd pick a clearing in the forest at dawn. No, a deserted beach by moonlight."

"Jervey"—Stanley hurried across the terrace—"I'm sorry I took so long. There was a line at every bar." He handed her the drink.

"Stanley, would you do me one more favor? Would you ask the orchestra to play a waltz?"

"Oh. Sure." He spoke stiffly, waited as if for further clarification, then turned. They watched him leave, every line of his body exuding resentment. He didn't have to make a request. As he went through the door, the orchestra moved into a waltz.

Jervey put her drink on the wall, faced Chance. "How about a Viennese ballroom?"

He regarded her seriously. "You are the beautiful young daughter of a noble house?"

"And you a young officer, about to go off and risk death in battle."

Slowly he lifted his arms, reached out. They touched, came together, his hand firm on her waist. The music took over, claimed them. They floated across the wide terrace, gliding, drifting, moving in extravagant curves and swirls.

I am celebrating, thought Jervey as she leaned back on his arm. I am celebrating a final foolishness for a very brief time, the space of a dance. She closed her eyes, hardly aware of her feet touching the ground. I will keep this, she thought defiantly. When I'm very old, scrabbling through memories for something special, I'll remember this. One beautiful, if fraudulent, waltz.

They were still dancing when the music ended. Gradually, reluctantly, they slowed, stopped. The moon slipped from behind a cloud and they looked into each other's faces.

"Tears in your eyes?" he asked.

"Yes."

"For me? I promise not to be killed in battle."

"I know. Not that."

"Why the tears?"

"Because the dance ended."

They stood very still. She knew she saw regret in his eyes, a sadness. Were they the eyes of Chance Crown or a young Viennese officer?

Very slowly he drew her to him. He held her head between big, weathered hands and, leaning down, he kissed her. It was a kiss that started gently, building in passion and ardor until it spanned the centuries between Oldport and

138

Vienna. When she drew back at last, it was like falling from a great height.

Silently they walked across the terrace to the door where they saw Roberta waiting for them.

Thirteen

· · · · · ·

When Jervey came downstairs the next morning, only Roberta sat at the kitchen table, drinking coffee and reading the Sunday obituaries.

"Odelle 'Aunt Shug' Greeley died," she said sadly.

"A friend of yours?"

"No." Roberta folded the paper, put it aside. "But anybody known as Aunt Shug must have been warm, wise, and a wonderful cook."

"Where are Emma and Milo?"

"Jogging. Emma's decided to lose weight, get her act together." She rose, a bit stiffly, poured a cup of coffee for Jervey, and returned to her chair. "Sit down, dear. Did you have a good time last night?"

"My feet hurt and I have a headache, Ma. What's more, tomorrow's Monday and the beginning of hell week. Remember how uptight Dad would be the week before a show opened?"

"How could I forget?" She leaned on the table, looked

140

squarely at her daughter. "Jervey, you've got to put everything else out of your mind."

For an appalling moment Jervey was sure that Roberta had seen her in Chance Crown's arms the night before. "What do you mean, Ma?"

"It came to me last night, looking at our little group, what idiots we've been, making all those wild conjectures about the bones in the mummy case. Thad, Abby, Lotte, Stanley never seemed more ordinary. By no stretch of the imagination could one of them have—"

"I know. I felt the same thing."

"We got carried away, I'm afraid. Of course, it was fun, but we'll never know the origin of those damn bones and we've got to let it go."

"And Sully?"

"Sully leaned too far out of that French door, Jervey. There was no support, no balcony. He was a big awkward man who lost his balance." She studied her daughter to make sure this had registered. "Now, is there anything I can do to help you this week? What about costumes?"

"It's under control. I'm going early tonight to meet with Tom Crain and set the lights."

Roberta leaned back, observed one long red fingernail. "Chance was quite a revelation last night. Who would have thought that—"

"Are there any English muffins?"

"Weren't you surprised?"

"No," she lied. "Thad warned me about him, hinted that there were some murky things in his past, that he isn't what he seems."

"That's too damn protective. He considers all of us his girls, needing his advice and counsel. I was thinking last night of all the women who have cried on his shoulder."

"Do you think he plays around?"

141

"Good heavens, no!" She laughed. "Jervey, I've not taught you much about men, have I? Particularly men who are obsessed with their own image."

"Their image?"

"The image they see of themselves in women's eyes."

"Do you think Thad was lying about Chance?"

"Let's say, sounding a soft but clear alert."

Jervey didn't want to pursue this further. She changed the subject. "Stanley gave me a present last night, a topaz and diamond pin."

"I saw it on your dress. I guessed as much. Congratulations, my dear. It's been ten years since Stanley picked a belle dame to worship. Prepare to have gifts lavished upon you. But beware."

"What do you mean?"

Roberta grinned. "Stanley's idols have a way of coming to unhappy ends," she teased. "No, I'm just kidding. But Polly Rowse, back in the sixties, left town under a cloud; Ellie Strang preceded Elissa and died of some obscure disease in Panama. You know what happened to Elissa."

"The pin once belonged to Ellen Terry," said Jervey glumly.

"Stanley has a great capacity for devotion. Not love, maybe, but asexual devotion. It has to go somewhere."

"It bothers me."

"He's harmless."

"I wonder why Abby and Thad didn't invite Fred last night. Snobbery?"

"I wondered myself. No, I don't think it's that. Fred adds nothing, brings nothing. He's neither attractive nor repulsive. A kind of cipher, poor lamb. But strangely enough, he's a good actor. He played my son in *Butterflies Are Free*. Remember? Onstage, he's generous, there for you. Offstage, zilch."

"I get the feeling that none of the men in my cast like each other."

"I wish your first directing job here had been with a happy cast. A good cast generally means a good show. A happy cast can produce real magic."

"Lotte seems to get along with everyone."

"Lotte's a survivor. You know, at one time there was a nasty rumor that her father had been a high-up Nazi officer. I'm sure that's all it was, a vicious rumor. She's a kind soul and if she enjoys being a woman of mystery, what the hell."

"Thank heaven, she and Abby get along."

"Abby! Can you believe that woman?" Roberta stood, stretched. "That house! That quite perfect, tasteful, welcoming house. She's a wizard, our Abby."

"You've got to hand it to her, Ma. When you think of how drab she used to be. I used to wonder why Thad ever married her."

"I didn't. I knew. The vision he saw of himself in Abby's eyes was irresistible."

An hour later, when Jervey was sitting on her window seat, staring at the weedy garden and thinking of doing a few aerobics, Emma arrived. Her small face shone with sweat; the red curls were damp. At first she stood silently beside Jervey, hesitating to intrude. At last she spoke. "My mother's present, we sent it Federal Express. You don't think it could have gotten lost, do you?"

"I'm sure she got it, Emma. And I'm sure she loves it."

Emma sat beside her. "We're going to leave in a few days, aren't we? Are you going to call and see if she's ready for me to come back?"

Jervey looked into the child's anxious eyes. "I'm going to call her, but I hope she's not ready. My apartment isn't exactly a luxury condo, but it's big enough for you and me. We'll do fine."

143

Emma scanned her face for some trace of dishonesty. When she spoke there was a flicker of hope in her eyes. "I can get to school and back on the bus. Sandra Gresham lives right near you and we can go together."

"Great. That settles it."

"If you give me a key, like Deirdre does, I'll be fine. I can come home, clean up, do my homework, and get things started for dinner."

"Sure you can. And if I get a part in a play or a soap, you can help me with my lines." She smoothed back a curl from Emma's forehead. "To be honest, I've never liked living by myself. It gets damn lonely."

For the first time since she'd come in the room, Emma smiled. "I guess we can kind of look after each other."

"Right."

"Is Roberta going off to California or somewhere to be in another play?"

"She hasn't said."

"I think she should stay here. She should stay here and marry Milo. Milo's a neat guy, Jervey. I mean he's not to be believed. They could stay here and Milo could cook and they could fix up the garden and—and—"

"Dance in the hall?"

"Yeah."

After Emma had gone to take a shower, Jervey mulled over what the child had said. Roberta and Milo. They had a great rapport. Roberta hadn't mentioned being lonely, but there must be times when she dreaded the years ahead, when she no longer would have the stamina for regional theater jobs. As for Milo, she was sure he wouldn't mind being a kept man. He would fill the bill with flair and aplomb.

She could avoid it no longer. Cautiously she allowed herself the thought that she'd held at bay all morning. Reaching for and finally achieving a cool objectivity, she reviewed the

144

encounter on the club terrace the night before. That flagrantly romantic waltz, feet hardly touching the ground, his firm hand at her back. The feeling of grace, of oneness, of flying. She stopped herself, weighed this against her capacity for self-delusion. "Pure theater," rasped a voice in her mind, "the Vienna ballroom bit, an old movie ploy. You knew that while it was happening and so did he. Together you wrote the script." But another part of her, voiceless, defiant, affirmed with eloquence the reality of the kiss, the joy, the dizzying lift of the heart.

She found the moment to talk to her mother about Milo that night after supper. It was Roberta's and her turn to do the dishes. Milo and Emma were watching TV in the library.

"Ma, I'm going to hate leaving you. How long is Milo going to stay?"

"He hasn't said."

"I must admit I like him."

"He certainly likes you. Despite your rather cool reserve."

"Ma, has he ever—I mean is he—what I want to say is—"

"Are you asking if his intentions are honorable, Jervey?" Roberta put down a dried plate and regarded her daughter with amusement.

"Exactly, Ma. To pay you back for all those questions when I was a teenager. Don't you know anything about him? What does his father do? Does he smoke pot?" She giggled. "Poetic justice."

"I don't give a damn about his intentions. He's a dear friend and he makes life fun and interesting and when he's around I feel young. Game for anything."

"Then, by all means, hang on to him. You might even consider—"

"Really, Jervey!" Roberta frowned. "I wouldn't want him to think I was after his money."

★ ★ ★

145

The next night Jervey arrived at the theater an hour early and Tom was waiting for her. She could see his trepidation as he watched her check the set from the back of the house.

"It looks good, Tom. Those curtains are perfect."

"Those African sculptures were buried back in the prop room. I thought since the old guy in the play's an archeologist he'd have stuff like that around."

Jervey looked at the solid wood images, one of an African head and one of a lion. He'd put the lion on the mantel, the head on the table behind the sofa.

"You're right. My Dad carved those years ago. I can even remember the show he made them for." She squinted, looked at the set more closely. "That table against the wall, right center, it looks kind of spindly compared to the rest of the furniture."

"It's all I could find. There's a Victorian table, but it's not long enough."

"My mother has one that would be much better. Also, a god-awful lamp that would be perfect on the desk. If you bring the truck to the house tomorrow, you can pick up both—oh, and the silver service."

Tom was a good enough set designer, but when it came to lighting he was stubbornly literal. The lighting of the show was simple, cut and dried until the final scene. Here, she wanted a subtle and gradual change, normal light moving into harsh overheads, giving faces a look of growing age, evil. At the same time, Tim, the son, lit from another source would take on the look of a Renaissance angel. Tom argued that this compromised the realism of the play.

"It's an important comment, Tom, the light, itself. It challenges our perceptions, how we see each other. A face can be young and beautiful one moment, old and evil the next. All by a trick of light. We're not suspending reality, simply extending it."

146

He looked at her with no sign of comprehension. "If you say so." He shrugged and moved off to the wings and his switchboard.

Chance was the first of the cast to arrive. They walked down the aisle together and climbed the steps to the stage.

"Is it time for me to abandon the tights and ballet shoes?"

"It is. We start dress rehearsals tomorrow night."

"Three dress rehearsals. Why three?"

Jervey quoted her father. "So you know that you know what you know."

She was aware of his uneasiness. She saw it in the tense set of his shoulders, the hand clutching the script. In the body language of relationships he was moving both toward and away. She'd never before seen him in a situation where he was unconfident or wary. Suddenly, she decoded the signals, knew what was bothering him. The simple fact that he'd kissed her. It was a moment of make-believe for a man not given to pretending. Dear God, she thought, he's worried that I might have taken him seriously. He's thinking I probably expect much more, maybe not something as farfetched as a commitment but a move in that direction.

She had an odd feeling of isolation, as if a door in front of which she'd been standing suddenly had slammed. She summoned all her resources as an actress and spoke with quiet conviction. "Chance, it's been a real revelation, watching you grow in this play. It takes some actors years to get as far as you have in a few weeks. I know it hasn't been easy, but I'm grateful for how much you've put into it. I just hope the experience has been worth it for you."

"It has. In many ways." He paused, then went on. "I guess you won't be staying long after the opening."

She could see he needed some final release. "I'm going back to New York on Monday." She noted no change of expression. "My agent's getting impatient," she lied. "And there are other reasons."

"It's a different life up there, isn't it?" His voice had a dull edge. "Fast moving, impermanent but exciting." He smiled. "No strings."

"Strings?"

"I read an article in a magazine in the barbershop. It was about attachments, relationships. It celebrated a concept called No Strings. An old phrase but still useful."

She didn't answer. There was no need. They heard voices, turned as Thad, Abby, and Stanley came down the aisle, trailed by Lotte.

Despite the fact that Fred was late and Jervey had to read his part in the first scene, things went well. So well it worried her a little. She didn't want them to peak too early. She surprised herself. She was able to lose herself in the play. If anything, her perceptions were even sharper. She was able to pick up the smallest flaws in timing, faulty moves, lost points, important moments not quite earned. She wondered if her newly relaxed attitude toward the cast had somehow freed them.

Lotte produced a *gugelhopf,* a Viennese coffee cake, for the break. They laughed a lot. They reminisced about the plays they had been in. Chance, outgoing, making contact with each of them, told stories in an impeccable Gullah accent. Thad warmed to him, perhaps realizing that he no longer need worry about Jervey's being interested in Chance.

Yes, she thought, they're finally coming together as a cast. It will work. And yes, an inner voice assured her, you are a director. She looked around the stage at the set, the library of the family in *The Spelling of Honour.* She stared out at the auditorium with its rows of empty seats. In a few nights, she mused, they will come together, cast and audience, and share an alternate world, the mysterious, wonderful alchemy of theater.

At the end of the rehearsal, they all left quickly. Chance was the first to go. Waiting to lock the theater, she turned down offers for a ride home, explaining that she'd driven her mother's car.

She'd turned off the stage lights and was walking down the aisle when she saw Lotte and Fred in the lobby. They seemed to be having an intense and quiet discussion. Then she saw Lotte hand Fred something that looked like bills. As Jervey slowed, Lotte turned and saw her. She laughed, one of her quick barks. Fred, pocketing the money, hurried from the theater.

"Caught in the act," said Lotte. She watched Jervey approach, shrugged. "My fatal flaw, Jervey. I play the horses. Fred handles my bets. It drives him nutty that I ignore his tips and still have bigger winnings."

"Good luck, Lotte."

They left the theater together, Lotte waiting while Jervey locked the big double doors. "It went well," she said, "the rehearsal. Don't you think?"

"Yes. It was a good one." Watching Lotte climb into an ancient gray sedan, she thought of the pastry box, Sully, a past remark that bothered her. She made no connection.

As she drove home in Roberta's car, almost as old as Lotte's, she remembered something else, a good bit more clearly. Someone, maybe Stanley, saying he'd seen Lotte giving money to the mysterious Keith. Ten years ago, it must have been Keith who shared her enthusiasm for the horses, placed her bets.

She envisioned Chance going home to his house in the woods, relieved to be free of all threatening entanglements. She pictured herself and Emma, bags packed, headed for New York. She knew that one day she and Roberta would look back and laugh at the mystery they'd created with prop-room bones.

A cat ran across the street just in front of her and she swerved to avoid it. She slowed, stopped the car for a few seconds. From somewhere an owl called. She shivered.

Fourteen

Later, when she thought about that week, the Tuesday through Thursday before Friday's opening night, it seemed a tangle of minor crises. There were the usual but critical errors in ticket reservations, a faulty faucet in the ladies' room, Lotte thinking she might be losing her voice.

After Tuesday's rehearsal Abby approached her with a petulant look. "Jervey, I know you want us all in dark clothes for that last scene, but I still think my dress needs something, a single strand of pearls, maybe, or a pin. I have this small diamond and ruby pin—"

"I don't think so, Abby."

Before she left the theater on Wednesday night, Stanley stopped her. "Jervey, you know I'm not a complainer, but something's been bothering me. Remember, at the end of the second act where I say, 'It's too late. It's too late for that'? Well, it's a crucial line and I think it's all wrong for Thad to cross over and mix a drink in the middle of it. It kills the point."

"It makes the point, Stanley. Trust me."

By Thursday night's pre-performance, even Thad was on edge. "Jervey, I know the end of the play needs that panoramic effect, all of us frozen in position, but I've felt from the beginning that my chair should be closer to center stage, not up left. The father's pivotal, like a deposed king surrounded by his court."

"The pivot has changed by then, Thad. Surely you know that. The son is the pivot. The focus has to be on Chance."

The day of opening night arrived too soon. Jervey was not pleased with the way it began. She came down to breakfast only to be greeted by grins from Roberta, Milo, and Emma. Roberta, as if bestowing an award, handed her a copy of the *Oldport Courier,* the local weekly. On the front page, a three-column headline proclaimed "Hap's Daughter Directs Play." Below was a picture of Jervey that had run in that same newspaper when she'd won the tri-state oratorical contest at age sixteen.

Jervey stared at the picture. "This is the absolute last straw." She sank into a chair.

"Look on the bright side," said Roberta. "I just heard that the box office is going great guns. Despite losing two Garden Club ushers they've been able to fill in with Girl Scouts. Esther Murray, who makes the best crab dip in the Southeast, is doing the opening-night reception after the play."

"I look like a—oh, Lord!"

"Startled doe," said Milo. "Charming."

"Tom Crain called," remarked Roberta. "The theater truck is finally repaired. He'll pick up those things you want for the set this morning."

"The table, some pictures, the lamp, sofa pillows, the tea service. Damn, I don't like to spring set changes on the cast at the last minute."

Roberta shrugged. "They'll rally."

152

Emma took the newspaper from Jervey and stared at the picture. "Jervey, you were cute," she said accusingly. "Even then."

"I was not cute! I was too tall, too skinny, too smart, and came from too weird a family."

Roberta leaned over, wound one of Jervey's dark curls around her finger. "You were cute as a bug's ear."

"Milo." Roberta turned to her friend, who, like Emma, was clad in a jogging suit. "Add coffee and anchovies to that grocery list. Oh, and some Granny Smith apples. I feel inspired to make a pie."

Milo did as instructed, folded the list, and rose. "Emma, let's be off. We'd better take the car. It's a long list."

Emma followed him to the back door, then looked over her shoulder. "Jervey, when you won that contest, what did you talk about?"

"All I remember, Em, is my certainty that I was going to get hiccoughs."

"Did you?"

"No," said Roberta, "I did. And her topic was titled 'Follow Your Dream.' "

Jervey was halfway through a bowl of cereal when she noticed her script on the table and, under it, one of her father's household ledgers.

"Ma, what are these doing in here?"

Roberta leaned back in her chair, her face a bit flushed. "Those? Oh, well I was talking to Milo about the structure of the play and I wanted to look up a line—"

"What about this?" Jervey paged through the ledger, a record of her father's household expenses ten years earlier.

"Jervey, really! Why this third degree? Incidentally, I just remembered, I not only have to get that silver service from the attic but it will need to be polished."

Jervey inspected her mother, who normally could lie with

consummate ease. "Ma, what's going on? What's my script got to do with Dad's old ledger?"

"Nothing, Jervey." Roberta rose, covered the butter dish and put it in the fridge. "I was just looking up an old entry."

"Ma." It was a command.

"Oh, all right." Roberta slumped into a chair, sighed. "Remember my telling you we should forget about those damn bones in the mummy case, get on with the show?"

"Clearly."

"Well, I still think so. But last night, I woke up with this nasty heartburn—it must have been from Milo's crab and avocado terrine with Pernod sauce. Anyway, I got up and took some Alka-Seltzer, but I couldn't get back to sleep. Jervey, do you believe that the subconscious is a vast computer of knowledge that we rarely use?"

"It's possible," said Jervey patiently.

"Well, lying in bed with my heartburn, I found myself thinking about that first production of your play, Hap's problems with the cast. Nothing specific except Elissa's tendency to be distracted, Fred's carrying the hostility of his character offstage, and so on. Then, just before I fell asleep, I could hear Hap laughing, then apologizing for his stupidity. Hap had thought Keith was awfully slow in picking up cues. At first he assumed it was the man's idea of how the character should be played. Then, bingo! He suddenly realized that Keith simply had a hearing problem. Hap never mentioned it to me again. The play opened, Keith was fine."

Reluctantly, Roberta picked up the ledger, turned a few pages. She pushed it in front of Jervey, pointed to an entry: "Keith, H.A. five hundred dollars."

Jervey looked at her father's neat notation. "April tenth," she said. "Three weeks before they opened."

"Obviously Keith couldn't afford a hearing aid, so Hap helped him." Roberta closed the ledger, pushed it aside. "I

154

wish I'd never eaten Milo's crab and avocado terrine, never had heartburn, never remembered."

"But you did."

"I remembered something else." Her eyes brightened. "When my Aunt Frances Bellows died, about six years ago—you were at college—my cousins asked if the theater would like the contents of her attic as well as her clothes and things. Lord, she had dresses dating back to the 1890s. They brought everything here because it seemed easier. Anyway, among her effects was an old ivory box, filled with bits and pieces of jewelry, some coins. I remember because I dropped the damn thing when I took the stuff to the attic. I swept it up, put the pieces back in the box, mostly single earrings and ugly pins and—"

"Ma, what are you getting at?"

"Aunt Frances wore a hearing aid. It could have been in the ivory box. When I swept up the stuff I could have missed it. And when Emma upset the mummy case, the hearing aid could have already been on the floor."

They both pondered on this. Jervey pushed away her cereal bowl. "I'm not going to think about it anymore, dammit. I've got a show to open."

"Agreed. There's another thing I don't want to think about, your leaving. But I know you've got to go."

"Yes."

"The Parmalee Players plan to offer you the job of permanent director. Total artistic control, like Hap."

"That's very flattering."

"When a board member told me, I showed no optimism. What's more, I didn't lie. I didn't say you've been asked to play Juliet at the Guthrie. Nor was I frank. I didn't tell him that a person of your talent could hardly be expected to bury herself in this town out of sheer love of theater."

"Ma, you know something? Something I've discovered these last weeks?"

"What's that?" Roberta's glance was light, careful, as if she sensed a fragile moment.

"I'm a director."

Roberta said nothing, nor did she move.

"If I hadn't come down here to do this play, I might never have known."

"I guess that's true, Jervey." Roberta pulled herself to her feet, stretched. "Oh, I learned something else, via grapevine. Chance Crown isn't the poor swamp rat he pretends to be. His Charleston grandma left him a tidy sum, as well as an old plantation on Edisto Island. He rents it to a rich Yankee conservationist."

"I'm not surprised."

"It appears," said Roberta, "that no one is what they seem anymore. And few perceive themselves as they really are."

"How do I perceive myself, Ma?" There was a thread of desperation in her voice.

Roberta, surprised, paused, took a step backward, and peered at Jervey, her face serious. "A presentable, together young woman, self-disciplined with no illusions and modest expectations."

"And what's the reality, the truth?"

Roberta lifted her chin with determination. "To begin with, beauty. You still see yourself as fourteen with bands on your teeth and no figure. Sometime between fourteen and eighteen you became a dryad. The awkward kid became a ballerina. All the features came together in that lovely oval face. I used to look at those long-lashed gray eyes, that straight little nose, that luminous smile, and wonder how I had spawned such a creature. No, don't you dare say I'm just talking like a mother. This is actor to actor, an honest assessment."

Jervey pushed back her chair.

"Wait. I haven't finished with the reality. Self-disciplined, yes. Together, no. The reality is a woman with wonderful, insistent expectations, so strong they frighten her."

"Are you finished?"

"For the moment."

"What about you? The perception? The reality?"

Roberta grinned. "What you see is what you get. You want to counterattack?"

"I wouldn't know where to begin. Ma, while you're in this omniscient mood, have you any ideas about Emma?"

"What do you mean?"

"She's happy here. I'll keep her with me in New York, but sooner or later, Deirdre will have a spasm of guilt and take her back. Take her back to God knows what miserable setup." Jervey fixed her glance on the table, fighting tears. "I can't face that."

"Emma can," Roberta said flatly. "Emma's going to handle whatever comes. She's vulnerable but she's a survivor. You can't keep her, Jervey. She's not yours. But we can give her something she's never had, a family, a refuge, a place to come to in the summers, at Christmas, an open door. Something unchanging, dependable.

"Now," Roberta shoved some dishes into the sink. "I'm going upstairs and, as Eliot says, prepare a face to meet the faces I meet."

Jervey washed the dishes, dressed, and then went outside to run. But when she reached the street, she found she was walking slowly, carefully observing each house she passed, as if she might never see it again. She noted the eighteenth-century plantation-type houses with their double piazzas, the later Victorian homes with wide verandas, all appearing to have carefully tended lawns and gardens.

Parents of some of her childhood friends still lived in a few

157

of the houses. Most of the friends had moved away, finding limited career prospects in Oldport. Buzz Creighton was a stockbroker in Chicago, Annie Briggs and her husband were both lawyers in Los Angeles. Billie, Alida, Trevor, Sarah, all gone. She paused at Trevor's place, almost a replica of her own. The old oak was still there, but the treehouse was gone.

The day was beginning on Main Street, people opening the small shops, a modest spurt of traffic. She crossed it quickly, taking care not to look toward the building where Sully had lived.

She found the waterfront busier. Boaters moved along the docks, some were washing decks. A charter boat with a group of frustrated fishermen seemed to be having engine trouble. Not far in the distance, near the fountain, Jervey saw Mary Ellen Bartlett pushing a double stroller. She started to call to her when she heard her own name yelled from above.

"Jervey! Hey, Jervey!"

She finally spotted him in a window over the marine supply store, leaning out and waving.

She waved back, called out, "Hi, Fred!" She moved closer, peered up at him, shielding her eyes from the morning sun.

"Come up for a cup of coffee?"

The words seemed to cut through the air and then hang there. She saw not Fred, but Sully, standing in his upstairs door, calling to her. She felt cold, leaden. She must refuse. She didn't want to face Fred at that point. She watched him motion to her. "The door's around the other side," he shouted. "I'll meet you there." Before she could answer, he'd left the window. Reluctantly, she went back past the entrance to the marine supply store. She found the side door just as it opened.

He looked keyed up, almost avid. "I thought you might help me celebrate."

"Celebrate?"

158

"I'm going to quit my job."

"Oh."

"Come on in." He started up a narrow, windowless stairway, lit by a single bulb. Longing to be elsewhere, she climbed after him.

He opened a door into a large, sunlit room with three windows facing the harbor. The furniture was arranged with military precision. A gray Naugahyde sofa and two matching loungers faced each other across a maple coffee table that held a neat stack of magazines. One wall loomed in bareness and another held a calendar. The one facing the windows was crowded with cheaply framed photographs. In a corner of the room a small Pullman kitchen seemed to cower.

"Very snug," said Jervey brightly, repelled by the room and the fact that she was there.

"It's the first time I've had my own place. I lived with my folks and then with my sister and her husband. But this is mine."

Jervey was surprised that a man in his forties would live with his family. Then she thought of Stanley.

"Cream and sugar?"

"What?" She looked at him blankly.

"In your coffee."

"Black, please."

He moved back to the door and turned the key in the lock, then went to the kitchen. She stood in the middle of the room, struck with sudden panic, like someone lost at night in a strange town. She tried to speak but had nothing to say. She made herself stir, walked woodenly to the wall of pictures. Maybe she'd learn something about him from seeing shots of his family.

There was no family there. Picture after picture showed Fred in a play: Roberta and Fred in *Butterflies Are Free,* Fred and Thad in *Long Day's Journey into Night,* Fred and Elissa in

A Streetcar Named Desire. Some of the plays dated back as far as fifteen years.

"A lot of pictures," he said, suddenly behind her. When she turned, she saw that he was sweating, that his eyes were very bright. She noticed, too, that he was wearing a suit and tie and rather flashy new yellow-brown shoes. His pigtail was pulled back neatly with a rubber band.

"Have a seat," he offered.

She went to the sofa and sat gingerly. He sat beside her. "You've worked with the Players for a long time, Fred."

"Yeah."

The silence seemed to go on forever. She felt skewered by the intensity of his gaze. He was too close. She could smell sweat and after-shave lotion. "You're going to quit your job." It sounded like some desperate announcement.

He reached in his coat pocket and pulled out a shred of newspaper. Without preamble, he read. "There's an immediate opening for assistant manager to train and develop for management with Regional Finance. The right individual can expect promotion to management within two years. Please apply in person to the office located in Oldport Mall."

He replaced the clipping in his pocket, rose abruptly, and stood before her, arms hanging limply, his expression unreadable. "Do I look okay?"

She stared at him, startled. What she saw was neither attractive nor repellent. But his eyes seemed even closer together and his hair—.

"Fred, you look fine, except for your hair."

The close-set eyes narrowed. "What's wrong with my hair?"

"Go get some scissors and a towel." She spoke with Hap's authority.

Some minutes later, snipping with skill and purpose, she mused on how she'd always liked cutting hair. She thought

160

of Roberta cutting Emma's hair and the splendid results. She knew that Fred's pigtail was entirely appropriate for his part in the play but could ruin his chances at Regional Finance. She'd tried to be airy but he didn't respond. He sat stiffly on a kitchen stool, glaring at the remains of his pigtail on the floor. Finally, she asked a question Hap would have deplored. "Fred, that first production of the play, how do you think this new one compares to it?"

He hunched his shoulders, shifted his weight and she narrowly avoided cutting an earlobe. He was in no hurry to respond. She'd decided to drop the matter when he finally spoke. "It's different."

"How?"

Again, no quick response. She went on cutting for several minutes. "No one's walking on eggs this time," he said. She didn't pursue it. For about fifteen minutes she worked on the lank, uninspiring hair, trying to give it some shape, if not style, a respectability.

"Lotte's better this time," he spoke suddenly. "Thad, too. Stanley," he laughed briefly, without humor, "Stanley never changes anything. It's by rote. If a cue's a little off, he looks like he could kill you." She went on cutting, letting him take his time.

"Chance—" he laughed again, "Chance Crown, what a piss-pot name! I thought you were upside down when you cast him. He's not bad."

"What about Abby?" She made it sound offhand. "Playing Elissa's part?"

He didn't answer.

"My mother says Elissa was a fantastic actress, not only beautiful, but so versatile—"

"Look, I've got to go." He thrust himself from the stool, pulled the towel from his shoulders. "I've got to get out to the mall. I've got an appointment." Leaving her standing, scissors

161

still poised, he strode across the room. He stood by the door, as if unaware of his rudeness, waiting for her to leave.

"Fred," she said quietly, "I hope you get the job. I really do."

"Yeah." He turned the key in the lock.

"You were brave to let me cut your hair. It looks pretty good, if I do say so. Well, I'll see you tonight and—"

"Yeah." He opened the door.

Fifteen

Going home, she jogged rather than walked, aware that she was trying to shake loose from the thought of Fred. She knew why she was feeling guilty. She pitied Fred. She was touched by all the pictures of Fred in plays, the only evidence of color in his drab life. She suspected that, despite the haircut, Fred wouldn't get the job at Regional Finance. But pity and empathy aside, she found it hard to like him. Worse, when he'd turned and locked his door, she'd had a moment of panic. Irrational, irrelevant, mindless panic. She thought, with a pang of the green suit, the polished shoes, the depressing apartment—"This is mine."

She understood his abrupt reaction to her asking about Elissa. Roberta had told her of his unrequited passion for that unhappy lady. What had happened to Elissa must still give him pain. Lord, what a mess, all the men in the play besotted with Elissa.

Roberta greeted her at the door with news that her agent had called. She also reported that Tom Crain had arrived with the theater truck and taken everything he needed for the set. "I had him take the mummy case as well," added Roberta. "Milo swept the bones into a trash bag and put it in the potting shed."

Emma showed her an elaborate kite that Milo had bought and which they planned to fly on the beach that afternoon.

Jervey didn't return her agent's call for another hour. She took a leisurely shower and dressed slowly. When she did call, Lynn Watson was terse and urgent. "Sol Horter wants you for *Eleanor's Song,* the young girl, no tryout. First reading next Wednesday. You've got it, Jervey. Not on Broadway, but not far off. Nice bucks. Get back here quick!"

When Roberta announced that she was meeting friends for lunch, Jervey didn't mention the call. Nor did Roberta. She gave her daughter one long look. "Are you going anywhere this afternoon?"

"No, Ma. I'm just going to read a good book and pretend it's not opening night."

"I'll be back early."

Alone in the house, faced with the opening, Jervey was tempted to throw herself on the bed and try to sleep. She resisted. Sleep at that point would be a form of flight. She wandered around the library, looking at Hap's enormous collection of books. She sat on the sofa and stared at the empty fireplace. She felt a heaviness, the way the air some- times felt as a storm gathered. She finally identified it as depression. She'd never experienced it before. It was all wrong. Opening nights were supposed to bring apprehen- sion, occasionally terror, but not a sense of impending doom. She hoped it wasn't an omen of things to come, a short circuit in the switchboard, a heart attack in the audience. Hap had never seemed depressed on opening night. Excited, a little edgy, but with a light in his eye, an air of anticipation.

She considered fixing some lunch, but the thought made

her nauseated. She weighed the idea of another walk, but her legs felt limp. Paging through old scrapbooks finally became tedious. She found herself slumped on the sofa, staring at the huge framed poster of Great-grandfather Parmalee as Richelieu, the corrupt French prelate. From above the mantel he seemed to look down on her with ecclesiastical scorn. Out of the blue, she found herself crying, tears pouring down her cheeks. She buried her face in a pillow and sobbed like a child. She cried for Hap, missing him with a sudden, wracking sense of loss. She cried for Sully. She cried because she couldn't rejoice in the fact that she'd been offered an important role in an important play with a first-class company. She cried at a sudden vision of herself far in the future, an aging actress living in a cheap hotel, waiting for one more part, at best a bit in a soap opera that would pay the bills. Not even a has-been but a might-have-been, disenchanted, left with a ragbag of memories of failed relationships with men she could barely recall.

When the doorbell rang, she stiffened, then pulled herself from the pillow. Hastily she wiped her eyes on her sleeve. She found herself running to the front door. She welcomed the intrusion, craved it. She didn't care if it was a Jehovah's Witness or a Jack the Ripper.

It was Chance Crown. He stood on the veranda, holding a Styrofoam cooler, filling up and dominating the space as always. When he spoke, it was with an uncharacteristic hesitance. "I brought some shrimp for your mother. She said she loved shrimp. Father Jake and I went out this morning to Brice Inlet and . . ." The words faded as he stared at her.

"That's very kind."

"She said she'd be here between two and five."

"She'd forgotten her lunch date." Aware of his scrutiny, she rubbed at her eyes. "A miserable allergy," she lied. She faked a sneeze.

165

"Come on in," she heard herself saying. "Would you like a beer?"

"As a matter of fact, I would." It was a wide smile. He followed her to the kitchen. "I would have shelled these, but I thought your mother might want to freeze them. I find that if you plan to freeze them, it's better to leave them in the shells." He walked to the window. "I like this room. It looks like a kitchen should, the center of things."

"Like the kitchen in your plantation house?"

He turned, eyebrows raised. "As a matter of fact, yes. How did you know?"

Jervey took a can of beer from the fridge, ripped off the top, and put it on the table. "It's a small town. With an endless grapevine."

They sat at the same moment, faced each other like trustees at a board meeting. She aimed carefully at nonchalance. "I'm glad the swamp rat doesn't live hand to mouth. Also"—she felt in control of things—"it adds mystery. I think that basically we're all a mystery to each other. And why not? It makes life more interesting, challenging."

"Exactly." He took a drink of beer. "That's why I didn't give you an immediate list of my assets and debits. Or," he went on, "a rundown of my triumphs and failures, likes and dislikes, certainties and uncertainties."

"Of course. That would take a lifetime."

"It should take a lifetime. So the mystery will last."

He observed the copper pots hanging above the cupboards. The ensuing silence didn't bother him. It was she who broke it. "Chance, are you nervous about tonight?"

He reflected on this. "Yes and no."

"What do you mean?"

"Communication. It's a dicey thing. As I see it, the audience will come tonight, take their seats, and wait for something to happen. They'll hope to be caught up, pulled into

166

another world, yet still have feelings they can identify so they can say, 'Yes, that's the way it is' or 'I never realized that before.' We either make this connection for them or we don't."

She tried to cover her amazement. "What about you as an actor?"

He laughed. "If I pass, hallelujah. If I don't, the worst that can happen is they'll say, 'What's that horse's ass doing on a stage? Send him back to the swamp.' " He frowned at his beer can. "You still heading back to New York?"

"Yes. I got a call from my agent today. I've been offered a very good part."

"Congratulations, Jervey." He sounded sincere. "Maybe I'll come to the big city to see your opening."

"Great."

He glanced at her, looked away. "What's it like, your life in New York?"

She was unprepared for this. She got up, went to the sink, poured a glass of water, and drank a few sips. "It's hard to describe. Busy, hectic." She was tempted to paint a state-of-the-art glamour picture, but her imagination went as flat as her voice. "Auditions, callbacks sometimes, temporary jobs to keep going."

"You must really love it. But, I guess it's your heritage, theater. You were programmed for it."

"You could say that. What were you programmed for?"

"I come from three generations of lawyers. The family firm's still going strong, my uncle, two brothers, a cousin. They'd say that's my heritage." He glanced out the window. "But I think otherwise."

Jervey smiled. "I can see you as a very old man, patrolling the marsh, squinting at and identifying a bird six miles away."

"You can?"

"And coming home to hold grandchildren on your knee and teach them about the wonders of nature."

"What about you? Will you teach your grandchildren how to make a classy entrance and a memorable exit?"

"I find it hard to think in terms of grandchildren."

"I'm sure there must be a man in your life."

She wanted to lie or at least hedge. If she said no, she risked his thinking she was not attractive to men or, worse, frigid. "You might say so."

"No strings, like the article said?"

"No strings."

He leaned back in his chair. "An actor?"

"No, a writer. A poet."

"He makes a living at it?"

"Of course not. He gets grants."

"Was he programmed for it?"

She suppressed a giggle. "No. His father has a Chevrolet dealership in Rochester."

"Then, good for him." He took a quick drink of beer, pushed back his chair and rose. "I've got to be going. By the way, any more thoughts about the bones in the mummy case?"

Jervey stood. "It was all a game, our playing detective. But it entertained Emma."

"What about Emma? I've wondered about her."

"I'm sure you have. No, she's not my illegitimate child."

"A relative."

"No. The daughter of someone I know in New York. Deirdre didn't want to mess up a new relationship with the presence of a strong-minded twelve-year-old."

Something like shock crossed his face. "She's a great little kid."

"Yes."

168

"I'll be damned." He walked quickly from the room, hurried through the hall, and out of the front door.

He would have left it at that but she called after him, "Thank you for the shrimp."

He lifted his hand, waved without turning. "See you tonight."

She finally allowed herself to take flight in sleep, lying on the library sofa under Pa Parmalee's chilly glance. She slept for several hours, hardly moving. At first she heard only dialogue, voices. Lotte saying, "How he loved sweets." Abby's voice, "The cake left over from the rehearsal . . . he kept the box." She dreamed she was playing Ophelia to Laurence Olivier's Hamlet onstage at Stratford and that she had no costume and a mind blank of all lines. She dreamed she was walking the streets of a strange town at night, not knowing why she was there or where she was going. Her own sense of terror and desolation waked her.

She heard voices from the kitchen. She looked at her watch, startled to find it was six o'clock. Oh God, she thought, only two hours until curtain time. She pulled herself to her feet.

Emma materialized in the doorway, a class entrance, a transformed Emma. She stood gracefully erect, head held high, red curls aglow. She wore an emerald green dress with a full skirt and short fitted jacket with small gold buttons, her new black patent shoes.

"Roberta found this," she explained, "while Milo and I were flying the kite. At Eloise's Boutique. Out at the mall. She got just the right size."

"Emma, you are truly a vision."

"It's not from a children's department," the vision assured her with pride.

"Of course it's not." Roberta entered, looking very smart in a gray wool dress with a wide gold belt Hap had bought

169

her in Mexico. She bore a tray of hors d'oeuvres, a pâté, some cheese and crackers. She put the tray on the coffee table, turned to admire Emma.

"Emma," said Milo, following Roberta, "you get a rave review." He gave Roberta a drink, offered the one in his other hand to Jervey, who shook her head. Emma, grinning with pleasure, went to the kitchen to get a Coke.

"Ma, that cooler of shrimp in the kitchen, Chance brought it. He said you told him you'd be here."

"I forgot. Anyway, you were here, weren't you? I'll put the shrimp in the freezer before we leave."

"An amazing young man, Chance." Milo took out his pipe and tobacco, changed his mind, replaced them. "Hard to categorize. Is he a good actor, Jervey?"

"I guess he's a natural. Strong concentration, energy, no self-consciousness. And imagination."

"Yes." It was a slow, reflective "yes" from Roberta. "Nothing seems to throw him. Have you noticed, Milo? An extraordinary man."

"He isn't a part of the contemporary scene, that's for certain. Talk about walking to a different drummer."

"Maybe he's from another planet." Emma, Coke in hand, spoke from the doorway. "Maybe," she continued, joining them, "he's been sent here by a higher civilization to help us save our world before it's too late."

Milo made room for her on the sofa. "I like that idea, Emma."

"All things are possible," said Emma with an enigmatic smile.

Jervey needed a change of subject. "Ma, I know we shouldn't talk about the bones or Sully or—"

"You bet your life we shouldn't!"

"It's just that I remember something about that night at

170

Thad and Abby's. We were talking about a memorial plaque for Sully and—"

"It's a wonderful idea, dear. We all feel—"

"No, wait, Ma, I—"

"Jervey, let it go. You've got to let it go. In about an hour and forty-five minutes you have a play opening. That's all that's important right now."

"Maybe," suggested Emma, "we should go back to discussing Chance. He sure is sexy."

"Maybe I'd better get dressed." Jervey rose.

She walked from the room, then, on impulse, came back and faced her mother. "Ma, you've always been an oracle when it comes to men. And I must say I've been entertained by the general endorsement of Chance Crown, but wasn't it you who warned me about men who were half in and half out the door?"

Roberta took a drink, cradled her glass in her hands, looked squarely at Jervey. "Yes, I did."

"Wouldn't you agree that Chance Crown is one of them?"

Roberta's smile was more enigmatic than Emma's, quite Etruscan. "This is something you must decide for yourself, my dear."

To divert herself she dressed with care. She even put on eye makeup, brushed her dark curls to a fine gloss. She slipped into her most expensive dress, a simple black sheath, and high-heeled black sandals. She borrowed her mother's double-drop pearl earrings and a white wool cape Roberta had worn some years before in *Idiot's Delight*.

Opening night. She sat on the edge of her bed, tried to breathe evenly. She thought of her father and grandfather, in that same house, facing all their opening nights. She thought of the hopes, the dreads, the sacrifices to bring live theater to a little podunk town. Hap and Orlando, and before them the first Pa Parmalee struggling to teach shopkeepers, librarians, lawyers, postmen, housewives, drifters, to amuse, enlighten, and transport in the name of entertainment.

She'd never forgotten her first big part in a play at the age of twelve, Hap's final words to the actors: "You're not a bunch of amateurs in a small-town show; you're the heirs of Euripides and Molière and Shakespeare. You're part of an unbroken line that goes back to the primitive man who first stood up at the campfire and acted out the words of the storyteller. You're theater." Later that night, alone in her room she'd written out what Hap had said, misspelling both Euripides and Molière.

When she went downstairs she could hear the others still talking in the library. Opening the front door, she almost tripped over a candy box, gold with a big blue ribbon. She knew at once it was from Stanley. With an uneasy feeling she took it inside and put it on the hall table. She didn't want to be the object of Stanley's strange, aberrant devotion. It was something she'd be happy to escape. Hot on the heels of these thoughts came guilt. Poor Stanley with his hopeless, harmless devotions. What did it matter? God help him. She wondered if it was he or his sister who set the table for breakfast the night before.

Sixteen

She drove to the theater in Roberta's car. The others would follow later. She moved past lighted houses where people were sitting at dinner or settling down for an evening of television. Not facing an audience. Not laying their lives on the line. She tried to think like her father: Poor devils, they don't know what they're missing.

The Parmalee Playhouse was aglow. The parking lot already was filling. She found a line at the box office window, a crowd in the lobby. Ancient Rob Roy Anders, who'd acted with Orlando in *St. Elmo,* stood proudly erect in his best suit, ready to take tickets. Ushers, the Garden Club volunteers and two Girl Scout fill-ins, stood with armfuls of programs. People she knew waved to her. Old Rob made a V sign and blew her a kiss.

She went backstage by way of the narrow cobblestone alley at the left of the theater, teetering in her high heels, climbing the wrought-iron stairway to the stage door. As always during performances, it was unlocked. She stepped into dimness, a hush. Tom Crain, sitting at the switchboard with his list of light and sound cues, nodded to her.

"You checked the set, Tom, the prop table?"

"Twice." He wasn't insulted. He managed one of his rare smiles.

In the ladies' dressing room, long, narrow with plain brick walls, Lotte and Abby sat at some distance from each other in front of a makeup table that extended to almost the length of the room. Lotte, costumed and made up, was drinking something, hopefully coffee, from a large Thermos. Abby was carefully applying false eyelashes.

"Abby, I don't think you really need those."

Abby wheeled and saw her. "Jervey, I just thought—well I know I'm not supposed to be glamorous, but, well, do I have to be totally drab?"

Jervey started to speak, stopped, reviewed the situation, remembering the dormouse. "No. But trim those lashes, Abby. Keep them short."

Lotte glanced at her, smiled vaguely, and took a sip of whatever she was drinking. She seemed distant, distracted, reminding Jervey of Roberta's observation that dressing rooms on opening night were cells of nervous chatter or sepulchral silence.

She didn't go into the men's dressing room. Before she reached the door, she heard Thad's voice. "I'm sorry, Stanley, but I have a thing about borrowing or lending."

"I didn't think you'd mind." Stanley's voice was even. "I was just brushing my coat. Say, Fred, you got a haircut. I just noticed."

"Jervey cut it. At my place. This morning."

"Oh." It was a weighted "oh."

For the next twenty minutes she sat backstage in the semi-darkness on a folding chair. She reflected on her father's

174

stubborn assumption that audiences arrive willing a performance to succeed.

When the cast finally emerged from the dressing rooms and
gathered around her, it dawned on her that she was expected
to give a brief pep talk. She looked at their drawn, opening-
night faces. Her mind went blank. Then she heard her own
voice, calm, nicely modulated, speaking with strong assurance.

"I want you to remember something. You are not a bunch
of amateurs in a small-town show, you're the heirs of Euripides and Molière and Shakespeare . . ."

A few minutes later, standing at the back of the full house,
she watched the last theatergoers hurry to their seats. She
listened to the sound of the taped music, Brahms, watched the
house lights go down. She felt an unexpected calm. Slowly
the curtain parted. There was a brief pause before the audience enthusiastically applauded Tom Crain's set. The design,
part Tom's, part Hap's, was impressive, the quintessential
library of an archeological scholar, lined with books, interest-
ingly if eclectically furnished, adorned with ancient artifacts.

Jervey, staring at the set, felt as if all the blood had been
drained from her body. Her vision blurred, cleared. She almost gagged. Standing to the left of the up-center door was
the mummy case. Stunned, suddenly terrified, she waited,
dreading each actor's entrance. Desperately, she told herself
that there was nothing to fear. The bones were a prop. There
was no crime. Still she waited for someone to come onstage,
find what they thought had burned in the fire. When had
Tom added it to the set? Late that day, behind the closed
curtains. No one would have seen it until now.

Hands clenched, she watched the actors. She waited for a
moment of revelation, a sudden lost cue, a misread line as one
of them had a moment of terrible discovery.

The play opened and moved forward without a hitch, just

as at rehearsal. It was as if the mummy case had always been there. She could feel the audience being caught up, drawn into the embattled family of *The Spelling of Honour*. She sensed their tension as the drama moved them, excited them, then offered release with a moment of humor. It was working.

Between the acts, she sat in the business office, looking at the flowers to be taken backstage for Lotte and Abby, mostly Abby. She saw her name on a particularly lavish arrangement, opened the small envelope and saw that it was from the cast. She greeted the two ushers who came in to get the flowers and deliver them. She felt weak with relief.

Watching the rest of the play from the back of the house, she was amazed by her cast. They went far beyond where she'd led them in rehearsal. There was total concentration, energy, a determination to get responses from each other. Abby actually turned herself into the sad, embittered daughter, every expression, gesture reflecting a wasted life. Lotte, the earth mother, hid old resentments in a spurious warmth. Stanley, an obsequious Iago, connived with relish. Fred had added a bitter self-awareness to his character, a barely concealed sense of guilt. Thad changed from a proud tyrant into a deposed and broken man. And Chance—Chance lit up the stage. With his height, hair gold under the lights, and clear voice, the contradiction of his appearance and the gentle, deprived person he portrayed was stunning.

Jervey could feel the involvement of the audience as the play moved to its inexorable end. No coughing, no stirring, total attention. She watched the final tableau, the actors motionless as slowly, barely perceptibly, everything changed. Faces aged, altered, revealed old dreams, old sins as the overhead lights grew harsher. Chance, alone, down center, was bathed in a golden glow, the outcast become archangel.

There was an initial hush, followed by nine rousing curtain calls. Slowly, still involved in the play, the audience rose and moved to the lobby for the reception. Jervey found the dimmest corner she could spot, partly obscured by a large potted plant. She felt limp, drained, overcome with gratitude. *The Spelling of Honour* was a difficult play, hardly a crowd pleaser. At worst, it could have been a pretentious flop. But it wasn't. It worked. She could tell by the faces of people flocking to the lobby that they'd experienced something special.

Before long she was discovered in her corner, greeted by old members, introduced to and congratulated by countless new people. Someone brought her a glass of wine. Roberta, Milo, and Emma, radiating delight, joined her.

Roberta gave her a quick hug. "How about that mummy case? See, no murder, no mystery."

"Ma, no 'I told you so's.' Please."

Eventually the cast appeared, all trying not to seem too pleased with themselves. Thad and Abby were mobbed by Accrolux friends. Lotte and Fred headed for the wine table. Stanley headed for Jervey, grabbed her in a tight embrace, and then stood proudly at her side. Chance, the last to appear, was at once appropriated by a group of chattering young females. Grinning, he waved to her from across the lobby.

It was a festive reception, with a lavish display of food and wine. Jervey felt that she'd been smiling for at least six hours, her arm weak from congratulatory handshakes, especially fervent ones from the members of the board. Finally, edging with difficulty through the crowd, she spoke to each member of the cast, affirming their triumph. It was not easy to make her way through the women encircling Chance but she finally managed. He was talking to a small perfect blonde, his face animated. Then he saw her across the blonde's head and stopped in midsentence.

She almost had to shout to be heard. "The communication was there. You made the connection."

"We made the connection. Thanks to our director." He

177

was searching her face in an odd way, looking for something. A loudmouth teenager pulled at his arm, forced him to turn. He looked back quickly at Jervey, but she was gone.

A garrulous, paunchy Accrolux executive was giving her advice on getting grants when Emma popped up at her side. "Roberta says we can hit the road."

A short time later, sitting in the library, shoes off, she was able to relax. Milo opened a bottle of champagne. Roberta produced cold Senegalese soup and a tray of sandwiches.

Emma made an announcement. "I believe I'm going to be an actress." Raising their fluted glasses, they drank to this.

Roberta joined Jervey on the sofa. "You're right about one thing, love. You're a director."

"Thank you, Ma."

"A good director," said Milo, "is a teacher, a psychiatrist, a father confessor, and . . ."

"A wizard," suggested Emma.

"I have a ways to go," said Jervey.

Suggestions came at once from Milo and Roberta. "How about Juilliard? No, Yale. No, Carnegie-Mellon. What about regional theater, learning on the job?"

At last Jervey announced that her agent had landed her a part in an important play with a good company. She was due to leave in two days.

Milo refilled their glasses, even Emma's. "Every director needs acting experience. By all means, do the part, make decisions later."

"You know," Roberta said as she took Jervey's hand, "I had a feeling he was there tonight."

"He was, Ma."

"Who?" asked Emma.

"Hap," said Milo.

Roberta rose, stretched, and strolled to the fireplace. "I just can't get over the cast. I knew they were pretty good actors, but they outdid themselves." She giggled suddenly. "And that damn mummy case!"

"Ma, did you tell Tom to put it on the set?"

"I swear I didn't. He probably saw it on the original prop list and decided it would dress up the stage."

"It nearly gave me a heart attack," said Emma. "When the curtain went up, and I saw it, I thought, Oh, wow, this will blow somebody's mind. That murderer's going to know that—"

"Except," Roberta broke in, "that there is no murderer, my dear. We all agreed that our conjectures about those bones were part of a game. Lively, fun, challenging, but a game. Tonight proved it."

"Exactly." Milo picked up a small sandwich, looked at it reflectively. "Roberta's right about the cast. They reached professional caliber. You know, it usually begins with one actor, sparking the others, lifting the performance. One actor, determined to prove that—"

"That he's not a murderer." Emma's stubborn words seemed to hang in the air like skywriting. Roberta glared at her, Milo burst out laughing.

Jervey poured herself a third glass of champagne, drank it, rose. "It's been a long day and a tough opening night. Good night, all."

Relaxed, fuzzy from the champagne, she lay in bed and watched the moonlight sift through the almost-bare branches of the chinaberry tree. She thought about the cast, how pleased and relieved they must feel. Did Thad and Abby go home to have a quiet drink alone or invite friends to join them? Did Stanley, wanting to share his triumph, find that his sister had gone to bed? The sister should have been there for Stanley's opening night. Or was she? No, if she'd come, Stanley surely would have introduced her. She imagined Lotte and Fred had gone somewhere for a nightcap. And

179

Chance? It was entirely possible that Chance had picked a blossom from that bouquet in the lobby and taken her home with him. Was this same moonlight filtering through a window of that little house in the woods, where they lay, wrapped in each other's arms?

Jervey was able to review this possibility with a laudable lack of jealousy or regret. She smiled with pride. Objectively, she wondered at what moment she had ceased to be a pitiful romantic. She couldn't pinpoint it, but she knew the milestone had passed.

You have the drive, she told herself, the determination, and apparently the talent to be a good director. You don't have a lot of important connections, but you have some. You're going to approach life now with single-minded ambition. If you're tempted to have an occasional fling, a little liaison, feel free. Lots of women in the arts had scores of lovers and still achieved greatness.

She slid to the side of the bed, put one foot on the floor to make the room stop spinning.

Seventeen

Jervey didn't wake up with a hangover. She felt full of purpose, in control, and just a bit cranky. The morning was overcast, a gray stillness. She showered, dressing in worn pants and a shirt, and, because she wasn't quite ready for human contact, dragged her suitcase from under the bed and began taking clothes from drawers and the closet.

She knew she was afflicted with the day-after-opening-night-letdown. She assured herself that she'd done a good job, that the play was a success and it was time to let it go. She'd appear at the theater tonight, watch one more performance, wish them all well, and then, as far as she was concerned, it was past history.

Finally, needing a glass of cold water more than anything in the world, she went downstairs. The kitchen was empty. Something aromatic simmered on the stove. Leaning against the fridge, she drank two glasses of cold water, then went to the library, carrying a refill.

Milo, impossibly suave in jeans and a yellow silk shirt, was ensconced in an armchair, reading a script. "Good morning." He looked up at her brightly.

It wasn't a particularly good morning, but she ignored this ritual hypocrisy. "Where are Ma and Emma?"

"Off to the shops. I believe to buy Emma a bra."

"A bra! She's only twelve years old. She's flat as an ironing board."

"Your mother mentioned a similar yearning when you were that age. Not a necessity but a rite of passage."

Jervey sat gingerly on the sofa, not hungover but expecting to be at any moment. "You reading a new script?"

"An offer from the Hartford. A lead."

"Great. Is it a good play?"

"Innovative." Milo closed the script, put it on the floor. "To slip into the vernacular, it breaks new ground, is resonant with contradictory truths, and assaults the mind and spirit."

"You're not going to do it."

"No." He stood, stretched.

Jervey took a long drink of water. When she spoke, her tone was airy, casual. "What are you going to do next?"

For a moment Milo's elegant face was impassive, then he smiled. "I'm going to break new ground and ask you why you don't like me." He sat beside her on the sofa.

Jervey gaped at him, put her glass on the coffee table.

"Come now, Jervey, you've been scrupulously polite, even warm at times, but my presence has been a trial for you. Child, I'm an old mummer. I can read the body language, vocal inflections, lack of eye contact."

She was not prepared for this. The control she'd felt earlier was slipping. She was getting a headache. She took a deep breath, looked at him, glanced away, then, opting for honesty, looked back at him. "I barely know you. You see, as long as I can remember, my parents have taken in theater waifs and strays, particularly my mother."

182

"Am I a waif or a stray?" Far from being insulted, he seemed amused.

"Neither." She looked at him squarely, reminded herself that she'd soon be leaving. Time was running out. Roberta would be furious at what she was saying, but she made herself go on. "You're too perfect, Milo, too stunningly 'British,' too talented a cook, too well spoken, too marvelous a dancer, too good with children, as adaptive as a chameleon."

"Which means you'd cast me as a . . ."

"Professional house guest." Jervey swallowed. "A few years back, there was a Colonel Maximilian St. John, ex-British colonial, ex-actor, charming as hell. He came every winter for a month or two and Ma would help him with his new piano monologues, the witty ditties he used when he sang for his supper. I remember Hap buying him a new suit. I know Ma lent him money. Occasionally he'd appear in one of our plays. From here he usually went to Palm Beach."

"Jervey, what are your worst expectations of me? That I'll be a permanent house guest? A perennial leech?"

"No," said Jervey coolly, "that you'll be my stepfather."

"Marry Roberta, run through her fortune with my extravagant ways and, when better prospects arise, abandon her?"

For a few seconds they both reflected on this dramatic if hackneyed scenario. "She isn't a rich woman," said Jervey.

"You forget I balanced her books. She's doing all right, but she'll have to be careful. I must say I don't like the idea of Roberta having to be careful."

"She's not good at being careful."

"That's why she'd be better off being married to me." He spoke with flat, undeniable candor. "If she agrees, I intend to keep her in the manner to which she should be accustomed."

Jervey stared at him, speechless.

"If you still have niggling doubts, I'll be glad to show you my latest bank statement and my investment portfolio." Head

183

cocked, he regarded her. "Dear Jervey, don't look like that. You have every right to worry about your mother. You know, you may not like me, but I think you're one helluva girl." He grinned. "And one helluva good director."

The front door slammed and Emma's jubilant voice rang in the hall. "Jervey! Guess what?"

They had a rather festive lunch. Milo's cassoulet was a marvel, enhanced by a Médoc claret of unimpeachable lineage. Even Emma ate like a hod carrier, mopping up gravy with crusty French bread. Jervey noticed that her little friend's posture had improved, small, flat bosom thrust forward in the new bra.

Finally, after patting her mouth delicately with a napkin, Emma gave Roberta a sly look. "You know," she said, "I've got this friend who never in her whole life has had to eat anything she didn't want."

Roberta raised an eyebrow. "I have this friend who has lived on junk food for thirty-five years. She still wears a size twenty-eight double A bra."

Emma's good spirits lasted until she followed Jervey upstairs and saw the open suitcase.

"Emma, would you like to take a walk? We could go down to this little store near the waterfront park. They have a lot of souvenirs, T-shirts and stuff like that. We could take things back to our friends in New York."

"No." The new bosom sagged. "That's all right. I think I'll just maybe stay here and read or something."

As she watched Emma leave the room, she felt a pain that seemed to fill her up and overflow. She wondered if this was what it was like to be a mother, watching a child's unhappiness and being unable to help.

She realized that she hadn't told Deirdre that they were coming back to the city and again went downstairs. She called from the phone in the back hall. After a garbled conversation

184

with a man who sounded half asleep and whose hostile voice was heavily accented, she reached Deirdre.

"Oh Jervey, it's you. Honey, I've been meaning to call, honest I have. It's just that so much has been happening. No, I didn't get the job with Belco, but I've heard of this much better—Luis, shut up, for God's sake! Luis has several weeks with the Cosmics, they need someone on drums and—"

"Emma's fine, Deirdre," said Jervey coldly.

"Emma? Oh, of course. I knew you'd take care of her, Jervey. What would I do without you? I mean, when I think of—"

"We're coming back to New York, day after tomorrow."

"Day after tomorrow? Oh, God, no! Look, Jervey, honey, it couldn't be a worse time for me. I mean Luis and I—oh, we're working things out, but if you could just maybe keep her a little while longer—"

"I'll keep her!" It was close to a shout. Jervey fought to control her rage. When she spoke, her voice was icy. "Deirdre, listen to me. You haven't called or written to Emma in almost a month. When we get back to New York, you'll call her every day, see her every week. You'll stop being a selfish bitch and give some thought to your child!" The lump in her throat was choking her. She hung up.

That night, she debated about getting dressed up to go to the theater. Realizing that she wouldn't be mingling with the audience, she put on a plain denim skirt, a white shirt, sneakers and pulled a sweater around her shoulders. She looked in on Emma, who, after supper, had gone to her room to read.

"Would you like to come to the theater with me, Emma?"

"No thanks." The little face looked pinched. "Tell the cast—what is it you say?"

"Break a leg."

"Yeah."

"I'll do that."

She went downstairs, waved to Roberta and Milo who were in the library watching a rerun of *Now, Voyager.*

"Will you be late, Jervey?"

"No, Ma. I'll be home ten minutes after the last curtain."

"If you change your mind, call me."

Driving to the theater she thought about her conversation with Milo, her misapprehensions about him. She admitted that even when she suspected he was a waif/stray/sponger/con man, she couldn't help liking him. It would be hard to dislike him. Maybe he seemed too good to be true, but he also was too damn honest not to be believed. She envisioned her mother planning a fall wedding in the garden. Except that the garden was a disaster area. Maybe Milo had a green thumb. Indoors or out, she'd have to make sure that Roberta bought a new dress for the occasion and didn't sail to the altar in a 1930s tea gown from some old play.

Once more the theater was aglow, humming with activity, the lobby crowded with people lined up for tickets. Jervey went down the narrow alley to the stage door. She looked at the warehouse to her left, almost a duplicate of the playhouse building. Hap had once thought to buy it and start a theater school. She wondered if it was for sale.

Tom Crain rose from his chair by the switchboard and approached her at once. "Look, I'm sorry about that light cue at the end of the second scene."

"What?"

"It was a few seconds late. I was having trouble with—"

"Tom, I know you'll fix it. You did a good job last night. We had quite an opening."

"Yeah. I was sure relieved."

"You had doubts?"

"No, no. Just a feeling. I guess it goes with the territory. Say, can I ask you a favor?"

"Sure, Tom."

"There's someplace I'd like to go tonight, a party for this friend. Would you mind locking up? I'd like to leave as soon as the show's over."

"You go ahead."

She moved about backstage, killing time. She greeted the stage manager, checked the prop table. She walked on the set, shrouded by the main curtain, lit only by a beam from a work light in the wings. As if drawn against her will, she went to the mummy case. She stared at it, thinking of all their wild conjectures. She saw that the side opening had been taped because of the rusted latch. She touched it, then with a sudden spasm of revulsion stepped back. How stupid, she thought. Then hands grabbed her from behind. With a half scream, she jerked away, wheeled around.

"Jervey, it's just me." Stanley stood close, his face pulled into a smile. "I was checking my props for the first act. That girl, that stage manager, forgot to put my glass by the lamp last night." The smile vanished. "I don't like to leave anything to chance."

The cast gathered before the first-act curtain and Jervey tried to combine a pep talk with a farewell speech. She told them how much she'd enjoyed working with them. She didn't praise but she affirmed. She told them to break a leg and before there was any response hurried through the stage door to the alley.

Again she watched the play from the back of the house, noticing that though the performance was smooth, the audience rapt, some of the opening-night drive and sharpness was missing. She would tell Roberta to mention this. Roberta would be taking over as surrogate director, on hand for the brush-up rehearsals.

Her gaze kept moving to Chance. His was the only performance that kept its opening-night edge. She continually was amazed at the way this rank newcomer had stepped into

187

a difficult part, at complete odds with his own personality, and managed a kind of brilliance. She suspected it was due to his extraordinary adaptability. She thought of her morning with him in the marsh, his enthusiasm, his appropriate silences. She remembered the dinner at the country club, his easy discussion of European museums. Wherever he was, he fit in, played the scene. The waltz on the terrace, lit by a trace of moonlight, was quite perfect. The kiss at the end of the waltz, an obligatory, dramatic device, was beautifully handled.

Midway through the third act she knew that she must leave. She needed air, space. She'd more or less said her good-byes to the cast. She left the theater, hurried to the car. By the time she reached Main Street, she felt more relaxed. She drove aimlessly, not ready to go home. For some reason she shrank from seeing Roberta and Milo in their companionable enjoyment of each other, and from quite possibly seeing again Emma's desolate little face.

She drove north beyond the town and turned down a dirt road that led to the beach. She pulled up where the road ended, between two dunes. There was no wind. Lights shone dimly from the windows of a few of the cottages. For a while, she watched the calm expanse of water, listened to the measured lapping of the waves. As always, it helped. She was able to empty her mind, let it drift. She closed her eyes, lost all sense of time.

A thought, abrupt and jarring, broke the spell. She was aware of time, of the fact that she'd promised Tom Crain that she would lock the theater. She looked at her watch and was amazed to find how long she'd been there. It was way past the final curtain. The audience and cast would have left; the theater would be unattended. As she drove back she realized that it really wouldn't matter if the playhouse was unlocked overnight. After all, this was Oldport and not New York.

The parking lot was empty except for the few neighborhood cars that were permitted to be parked there overnight. The playhouse was unlit. Someone had turned off the lights and perhaps locked up as well. She had no idea how many people had keys. Tom Crain, of course, and the stage manager. Stage managers always had keys, as did the chairman of the box office and some board members.

She walked to the big double doors and found them locked. She'd been derelict but someone had had their wits about them. She decided to assuage her guilt by checking the stage door.

The narrow alley, with its three streetlamps at beginning, middle, and end and its uneven cobblestones, looked like a Sherlock Holmes set, shot in black and white. But nothing menacing moved in the shadows; there was no eerie background music. As she climbed the steps to the stage door, she decided she'd better call Roberta and explain why she was late.

The door opened at once. Whoever had locked up had been less than careful. The stage door could be locked only from the inside, so she'd have to see to that and then leave by way of the lobby and relock the main doors.

The bolt slid in place without a sound. She paused to look around the backstage area, lit as always by dim work lights. Nothing, she thought, is emptier than an empty theater. Just a short time ago, it had been filled with people, with the excitement of what was happening onstage, a particular magic.

She moved past the upstage wings, the switchboard, to head down the steps to the auditorium. As she reached the right center door to the set, she slowed, listened. She thought she heard a sound. A sound from just beyond her, on the set. She stood completely still. It crossed her mind that she should be startled, apprehensive. She was alone in a dark theater that

189

she'd supposed was empty. But someone was on the set, someone making a sound. An odd, scraping sound.

As Jervey opened the set door, something crashed, fell heavily, shook the stage. She jumped back, sure that all the scenery was falling. Then she saw what it was. The mummy case lay on the floor in two parts, each gaping emptily. Abby was staring at it. She leaned over, as if unable to believe what she saw or didn't see. In her right hand she held a pair of scissors. Her face was dead white, blank.

"Abby?"

She raised her eyes slowly, finally gazing at Jervey as if trying to place her. She had the look of an actor who has forgotten all lines. Stunned, Jervey waited. The face lost its blankness, some color returned. Within seconds it was the smooth, familiar face, the social face, Abby Egan, president of the Accrolux Wives Club.

"Oh Jervey!" She laughed with relief. "You really scared me, coming out of nowhere like that." She glanced at the mummy case, laughed again. "I'm afraid I bumped into that. Lord, I hope I didn't ruin it. Frankly I didn't like coming back to this empty theater but Thad and I got all the way home and I discovered I'd left my watch. I didn't tell Thad, just let him go off to bed, but I had to come back. My watch. I don't wear it onstage, of course, because I can't see that character being concerned with time. It's something I'd hate to lose. Thad gave it to me for Christmas last year and . . ." The words faded away as she followed Jervey's gaze to her own hand still clutching the scissors. She opened her fingers, dropped the scissors at once.

"Are you leaving soon, Jervey? We'll hate to see you go. You've been an inspired director. We all agree on that."

She turned, moved to the mantel, touched a brass candle holder. "We used this in *I Believe You* years ago. I played the maid." She picked up the elongated wooden head. "And Hap made this. Oh, your father was an incredible man. He could do anything, sculpt, paint, design." She walked back to Jervey, still holding the head. "He always signed his work with that funny little—what did he call it?—cartouche. I have an oil painting he did. Maybe you saw it in my upstairs hall. It was for that English comedy. I can't remember the name. I played the housekeeper. I admired it and he gave it to me." She inspected the carving. Jervey stood frozen.

"There it is!" Abby had turned the carving upside down, was pointing to something on the underside. "Look, that's it, his mark." Abby held it toward her and numbly, without thought, Jervey leaned in.

The carving swung toward her with a savage swiftness. She tried to duck, pull back, but too late. She felt a crashing pain, seemed to hear her very skull resound. There was a spinning darkness as she fell.

It was so quiet. Still spinning in darkness, she felt wrapped in silence. She felt something else, something blinding one eye. It was thick and wet and she knew it was blood. Her mind inched toward consciousness. She dared not move. If she moved she would be hit again. She thought of the scissors. Abby. She'd already killed twice.

Jervey peered through the one eye not filled with blood. She saw Abby's feet in flat brown shoes. They didn't move. Nothing happened. For an eternity Abby did nothing. She simply stood there.

The sound was as sudden as a clap of thunder. Abby's feet jerked back, then sideways, then stopped. The sound was louder. She couldn't tell where it came from, a determined knocking. Someone was there. Thank God! Someone had come! Silence.

Abby's feet moved out of her sight. She could hear the soft tapping as they hurried downstage. Jervey waited, willing

191

whoever had come to get inside. But they couldn't. They had no key, no—

Abby was making strange sounds, a whining cry like a netted animal. Jervey heard something creaking, then the sharp report of wood hitting wood. The trapdoor just above the curtain line.

Hands like a vise grabbed her ankles as Abby pulled her forward. She was being dragged downstage, not sure she could move arms or legs, knowing she couldn't fight back. Abby's hands were on her shoulders, pushing, shoving from behind. Then she was being thrust down into black darkness, falling, falling to somewhere below. Her head rang as it hit the cement floor. She tasted dust. Scattered boards bit into her back.

Her whole body vibrated with pain. She was suspended in pain. She struggled to think, to clear her mind. She must fight for her life. Abby would get rid of whoever had knocked. Get rid of them and then come to get her. Abby would have to kill her. She felt a crawling on her arms and legs. Something furry, oily, ran across her face, a rat. She screamed at last, a muffled sound. The place was alive with roaches. She shuddered violently. Half crazed with fear, she kicked, flailed her arms. Her stomach heaved at the rancid smell. She lashed out again and again, half crawling on her belly. She screamed, yelled desperately, hoping that whoever had knocked would hear her. Nothing. No sound.

The slit of light was barely visible. Disoriented, not knowing which way she faced, she squinted at the thread of brightness. She remembered . . . she remembered! Elves, the three elves going down the trap door. She and the other two elves, crouched over as they hurried to the opening in the side of the theater. Yes! Yes, they'd crawled into the alley, run up the steps to the door, hurried to the wings, and miraculously reappeared onstage.

192

She pulled herself toward the light, felt a nail tear at her leg. Blood blinded one eye. It seemed hours before she reached it. There was so little light. So little, only a crack where the board had been nailed to block the opening. She wanted to cry, to give up, let go. Instead she grabbed the board, pulled. The nails held. She pulled again, tore at it. Just as her strength ebbed, she felt it come away, come loose. She dislodged it, lay gasping.

The night air flowed in. Trembling with relief she pulled herself through the opening, dragged herself out into the night, gulping the air, and lay at last on the cobblestones. It was several seconds before she could even half lift her body. She tried to brush the blood from her eye. She peered toward the other end of the alley, the front of the theater. No one. In terror, she looked back toward the stage door. No one. Dizzily she sat up, waited a few seconds. With an enormous effort she pulled herself to her knees. Her head was clearing. She could feel some strength in her legs. Controlling her panic, steeling herself, she hoisted herself up and stood at last, shaky, lightheaded but on her feet.

The tall shadow had moved beyond the first streetlamp and was coming toward her. She staggered, opened her mouth to call and no sound came. She recognized the walk, the angle of the head. He was running.

"Thad!" It was half scream, half sob. She called his name again, engulfed with relief. Seeing her under the streetlamp with her bloodied head he slowed, approached her with disbelief, stood shocked. Then his arms lifted and he reached out, grabbed her, held her against him. Head on his chest, eyes closed, she gave a long, shuddering sigh.

"It's all right, Jervey. It's all right, dear." His mouth was against her ear. She could feel the warmth of his breath.

"Abby"—she gasped—"Abby tried to—"

"It's all right."

He didn't understand. She strained to see him with her one clear eye. "She tried to kill me, Thad!"

Frantic beyond thought or reason she thrust herself from him. She stumbled, her legs limp. She swerved, began to hobble down the alley, knowing only that she dare not stop. She could hear him following. She tried to push the blood from her eye, forced herself to go on. But as she reached the second streetlamp, hands clutched her shoulders, swung her around. Half blind, she stared up at him.

It was an unfamiliar face. The harsh light of the streetlamp showed a mask, cold and unyielding. No dark eyes, filled with compassion, just cavernous sockets. It's the light, she thought staring at him, only the light, she thought wildly.

"Thad!" It was a choked, despairing cry. Not true! she screamed inside even as his hands moved to her throat.

"No!" She jerked back, tore at his hands. Her knees were buckling. The hands tightened. She fought to breathe.

It was a shot, then a bellow, a roar. She thought it was inside her head as she spun again into darkness.

Eighteen

She squinted up at her mother's face. Roberta looked old, gaunt. Roberta always said that fluorescent lights, particularly overheads, were supremely unflattering.

"Ma?"

"Jervey?"

"She'll be all right, Roberta." Doc Saunders's voice was soothing. "As I said, head wounds always bleed like that. From the tests, there's an indication of a slight concussion."

Slowly, carefully Jervey looked around. She was lying flat out in what seemed to be a hospital examination room. Doc Saunders, short, stout, his thick gray hair on end, wore a smile as wide as Roberta's.

"Ma?"

"Right here, darling."

"Ma, Thad, Abby—"

"I know."

Early in the afternoon, following a few more tests, she was released from the Oldport Memorial Hospital, built after the

195

coming of Accrolux, and driven home by Roberta, who tactfully asked no questions. Milo and Emma were at the front door, waiting. Without words, each put their arms around her, holding her close for a few seconds.

It was only after she'd had a long bath in the big clawfoot tub, washed her hair under the shower, and put on clean clothes that questions were asked.

"Ma, I heard a shot last night. I know I heard a shot."

Roberta, sitting by the window, seemed herself again. The haggard look was gone. "Chance. He fired into the air." She watched Jervey sit on the side of the bed. She inspected her closely before she went on. "When you didn't come home after the show, I got worried. It got later and later. I phoned every member of the cast and they knew nothing. I even talked to Thad. I guess that's what alerted him. He must have discovered that Abby was gone and tore back to the theater. Milo and Chance got to the parking lot at the same time. It must have been only minutes after Thad. They found the front doors locked, headed down the alley. Apparently Chance, following some instinct, brought the gun he kept in the truck. They saw you struggling with Thad. Chance fired the gun."

"Thad, Abby—"

"They're in custody, Jervey. As soon as Abby heard the shot, she ran out of the stage door, saw you in the alley. Milo says she put on quite an act, the innocent bystander bit. Milo went in the theater and called the sheriff."

"Thad." Jervey closed her eyes. "I still can't believe, don't want to believe . . ."

"I know. Strong, caring, compassionate Thad. Pillar of strength, virtue, and all good things. It hurts. Betrayals hurt, Jervey. They hurt more than anything." Her sigh was a long, ragged sound.

"Jervey?" Milo stood in the open doorway. "The sheriff is

196

downstairs. He wants to know if you feel up to talking with him."

"Sure. I'm fine."

"Last night your mother and I talked with the sheriff, told him all we knew. Roberta explained about the mummy case, how it happened to be in the attic. We told him about the hearing aid, the fractured bone, Sully talking in front of the entire cast. He knows the whole story."

Jervey found Sheriff Elkanah Sparkman in the library being grilled by Emma.

"But have you ever killed anyone? I mean, like on a raid or stakeout?"

Seeing Jervey, El Sparkman rose with a reprieved look. "Jervey, I hope you don't mind. I won't keep you long."

"I'm fine, Sheriff. Emma, I think Milo could use your help in the kitchen."

They watched Emma depart reluctantly, then sat, Jervey on the sofa, the sheriff in one of the lounge chairs. A tall, lanky man with a cheerful, rather horsy face under a close crewcut, he wore a neatly pressed uniform and held a small cassette player.

"Jervey, if you could just tell me what happened from the time you went back to the theater last night."

She watched him switch on the recorder. His homely-attractive face was expectant but patient. She told him, trying to remember every detail. Her voice was calm, her account careful. Every step hurt. She felt as if she were walking on nails, but she described it all, right up to the firing of the shot. Spent, torn, she watched him turn off the machine, eject the tape, put it in his pocket, and then slip in another tape.

"I think you have a right to hear this," he said. "It's against all regulations, but dammit, you have a right." He fixed her with a thoughtful glance, chewed his lip. "You know, they came in like lambs to the slaughter. No yelling about their

197

innocence, no demands for their lawyer. Hell, he's a lawyer, himself. You know, he didn't say one damn word. Just sat in my office like a zombie. It was the wife that talked. Man, but she talked! Jabbering away, jumping from one thing to another. She kept looking at him. She'd stop, wait for him to say something, then she'd be off again, talking a blue streak, not making sense. Then, all of a sudden, she calmed down. She stared at him for a long time. Then, out of the blue, she confessed. She said she'd been having an affair with this Keith fellow. She'd been crazy about him, her first love and all that. On the last night of the play, just before it started, she went to the parking lot to get something from her car. She saw Elissa Dowell and Keith putting Elissa's suitcases in his car, saw him kiss her. She went wild with jealousy. After the show, she hid in the prop room, waited. Keith was always the last to leave except for the stage manager, which was Abby, herself. He always took a shower, and that's where she killed him, in the shower with a pair of scissors from the prop room. She dragged the body out and put it in that mummy case. She was afraid someone might come in and surprise her. She drove Keith's car to a street on the south side. She had to make it look like he'd left town. When I asked her why she didn't put the body in the car, she said she planned to do that, after the party when there wouldn't be the risk of running into the people who used the parking lot. But after the party, there was no mummy case, no body. She said that's why she started the fire. She knew it had to be in the theater somewhere. But the fire, as we know, was caught early by old Sully. It didn't do much damage. Still, there was no body, no investigation.

"The big change came after I asked her if she was willing to sign a confession. For a long time she didn't say anything, just sat there staring at her husband. Him, he never even

198

glanced at her. He sat cool as a cucumber, like a judge or a priest."

He held the cassette player on his knee, pushed a button, put it on the coffee table. "This is the part I think you should hear."

At first Abby's voice was inaudible. There were broken words, the strange netted animal sounds that she made when she was dragging Jervey to the trap door. Several seconds of silence. Then came a clear voice, the voice of a woman appalled, unbelieving. "Thad? You haven't said a word. Thad, look at me. Didn't you hear what I said? Why are you just sitting there? You missed your cue, Thad. This is where you say, 'She's doing all this to save me. It's just as she said, but I'm the murderer.' Pick up your cue, Thad!"

Abby's voice slid into a lower key. The words were sharp, corrosive. "Damn you, look at me! You'd do it, wouldn't you? You'd let me lie for you, go to prison for you! Because the great Thad Egan is so important. Even that night, after you'd done it, when I blundered into the dressing room, the shower room, and saw him lying there, all that blood and water going down the drain, you sat there and cried. I remember your crying. It killed me to see you cry. 'I had to save her from him,' you lied. 'Then you looked at me with those wonderful eyes and you said, 'Oh, Abby, do I love too much?'

"I pushed Sully to his death for you. I was the one, Thad. I was the one who loved too much."

"Oh God, I wanted you to save me, Thad. I wanted you to come to my rescue, to show I meant something to you. Oh, I know, I know. You married me to shut me up, but I thought, I hoped—didn't I matter to you? I tried so hard, the perfect wife, the perfect house. Didn't I matter?"

There was silence from the tape except for the sound of

199

Abby breathing. Jervey prayed that there was no more. Horrified, she wanted to run from the room.

The sheriff rewound the tape, ejected it, and put it in his pocket. Jervey watched in silence. What she'd just heard was as shattering as what had happened at the theater. She fought for some vestige of calm, some control.

The sheriff rose, spoke matter-of-factly. "You know when I asked what they did with that poor fellow's car, well it turns out they sunk it in the marsh, way up just south of Wadmalaw." He rubbed his chin, ran a hand over the stubble of his hair. "Roberta says you plan to leave for New York tomorrow. We may need you to come back and testify. This case is a real can full of worms."

"Just let me know."

"I swear, life is funny. If Abby hadn't been so damned curious, hadn't tried to check that mummy case—Roberta says it had been onstage since Friday—hell, we might never have known."

Jervey followed him to the door. He looked at the bandage on her forehead. "Doc says you're going to be fine."

"That's right."

"Thad Egan," he mused, "who would have thought! A damn good actor, looked like a movie star. Thad Egan! I was in a show with him once." He grinned. "Does that surprise you?"

"I guess it does, Sheriff."

"Yeah. I was in the Blue Dolphin one night, years ago, having a beer with some buddies, when in comes Hap. He sat at the bar and cased the joint for quite a while, then all of a sudden, he comes over to me and says, 'El, I really need you. Have you ever read any Shakespeare?' Next thing I know I'm up on that stage, feeling like a jackass and having a whale of a time."

Jervey smiled, opened the door. The sheriff patted her

shoulder, walked to the veranda steps, turned. "You know something else? I wasn't half bad."

She found Roberta, Milo, and Emma at the kitchen table. Roberta looked at her anxiously. "Has El gone?"

"He's gone."

"Did you know he was in a play once? *A Midsummer Night's Dream.*" She laughed. "Lord, you should have seen those bony legs in tights!"

"Chance called twice," said Milo, "to see how you are."

"I thought surely he'd be here." Roberta plucked at the bowl of marigolds on the table. "He was so concerned, stayed at the hospital all night." At Jervey's lack of response, she changed the subject. "I think we'd better do something about canceling the run of the play. At least put a sign on the door of the theater, have some flyers printed."

"No." Jervey spoke firmly. They all stared at her. "No," she repeated. "The Parmalee Players have never canceled a performance. Never." She turned to Milo, managed a soft smile. "Don't you agree, Milo?"

Milo read both the smile and the question. He sighed, returned the smile. "You only play weekends, don't you? That leaves four days to learn it and to rehearse."

"Of course!" Roberta grabbed his arm. "Milo, you could do it easily. God knows, you're a quick study. Remember that time in Alabama, when Joe Haverty got sick during *My Brother, My Foe*? You learned the whole part in a day and a half."

"Of course," chimed Emma.

"Well, I'd rather go skydiving," said Milo, "but I'll give it a whirl." He glanced at Jervey. "Will you be playing the daughter?"

"No. Emma and I take off tomorrow."

"Now that is a problem." Roberta frowned. "Who the hell could we get? Jervey, maybe you could—"

"No."

"Then what on earth will we do?"

"It's too late to go to church," observed Emma, "and the Blue Dolphin bar is closed on Sunday."

"In my mother's immortal words," said Jervey, "we'll improvise."

Callers began arriving as if there'd been a death in the family. Virginia Spinner brought a baked ham, Lorena and Bubber Hanson a shrimp casserole and two six-packs of beer. Other offerings included four dozen sandwiches, a lemon meringue pie, a seven-layer salad, several pounds of barbecue, a huge chocolate cake, and a bottle of bourbon. No one stayed more than a few minutes. The remarks were concerned, a little embarrassed.

"We just heard what happened. A real shock."

"Hope you're all right, Jervey. A terrible thing."

"Let us know if there's anything we can do."

The last to arrive were Lotte, Fred, Stanley, and a stranger. They didn't bring food, but Stanley, beaming importantly, introduced the newcomer.

"Jervey, Roberta, Milo, this is Evelyn Carroll. She's just been here a few weeks, lived in Abbeville. She's taken a position with Accrolux."

"I'm just a secretary," said Evelyn in a small voice.

"She's an actress!" announced Stanley, aglow with the news. "She's done parts in Abbeville, Greenville, and Anderson."

"Really?" breathed Roberta.

All attention was on Evelyn, who stood like a rabbit surrounded by hawks. A frail, wispy-looking woman in a filmy flowered dress, she pushed nervously at the cloud of pale hair surrounding her plain little face. "He's exaggerating," she said. Her voice was soft, breathy.

Roberta beamed triumphantly. "Let's all go in the library."

She herded them forward and, as she started to follow, Jervey drew her aside. "Ma, cut it out. That voice won't reach beyond the first row."

Roberta patted her cheek. "Let's wait and see."

Milo brought a few more chairs to the library and Jervey, with apprehension, waited for her mother's next move.

It was Milo who set the tone. With the right mixture of humor, style, and modesty, he explained that he'd be joining the cast and would appreciate their help.

"You can count on us," said Stanley.

Lotte looked at him as if he were a celestial vision. "How fortunate we are."

Fred was practical. "We've all got our scripts in the car. What do you say we have a read-through?"

Several minutes later they were back in the room, holding scripts they didn't really need, seated and ready. Jervey brought hers from the hall, started to give it to Milo, stopped. "Milo, would you mind sharing with Lotte?" She turned to Evelyn and spoke with Roberta's tone of velvet coercion. "Evelyn, would you help us out and read the part of the daughter?"

"Sure," whispered the girl.

"Catherine. Beginning on page two. I'll read Chance's part."

They read. Jervey somehow had known Milo would be good and he was. His approach was different from Thad's. She could see him giving the part more depth, a sharper mentality. It would heighten the final tragedy. Even physically he changed. Sitting on a straight-back chair, his body took on a different character. The British elegance was gone, replaced by a stolid authority. Jervey could sense the response of the cast, their surprise, enormous relief.

The shocker was Evelyn. Voice almost half an octave lower, she read with intelligence, feeling her way with what seemed an intuitive understanding of the blighted Catherine. At the end of the reading, Roberta and Jervey exchanged exultant glances.

"Evelyn," said Jervey, "how would you feel about joining our cast?"

"How would I feel? Do you mean it?"

They reread the play. It was arranged for Milo and Evelyn to meet with Roberta at the theater two hours before each rehearsal for the next four days. Roberta would block the action, give help if needed, and handle the actual rehearsals with the rest of the cast.

Suddenly it became a celebration. They all milled around in the kitchen. Roberta set the big dining room table. The cornucopia of food from well-wishers was arranged on the long hunt board. Milo produced bottles of wine. When they all were seated and the wine was poured, Lotte suggested that they hold hands and say grace.

Milo obliged with a grace reminiscent of the one offered by the grandfather in *You Can't Take It with You.*

"Well, God, here we all are. We've been through some rough times in the last twenty-four hours, but things are looking better. Jervey's okay and we're grateful for that. Evelyn's joined the cast and so have I. Roberta's going to take over as director and we'll all do our best. Jervey and Emma are going off to New York, but we know they'll come home for Christmas. That's about it, God, except to say that we're thankful for the ham, the cake, the shrimp casserole, the pie, the sandwiches, the Peedee Pilau—"

Noticing Roberta's raised eyebrow, he intoned a reverent "Amen."

"What about a toast?" asked Emma.

No one spoke. Jervey thought suddenly of small theater groups like theirs, all over the country, performing in high school gyms, parish houses, converted barns, with nothing but the will, often against all odds, to open the show. She stood up, looked carefully at each face, lifted her glass. "To theater," she said.

After the sumptuous meal, much wine, much talk and, finally, laughter, the celebration ended. Roberta, Jervey, Milo, and Emma stood on the veranda and watched their friends leave.

"Bedtime, Emma." Roberta tweaked a red curl.

"Good night, dear ones." Milo saluted them. Whistling to himself, he headed for the barn apartment.

"Jervey?" Roberta spoke from the door.

"Ma, you and Emma go on. I'll be up in a minute."

She leaned against a pillar, breathed in the cool night air, smelled the beginning of autumn. She looked out toward the town, silent, dark, ready for sleep. She felt a heavy tiredness, as if she'd walked too far, seen too much, painfully stretched the boundaries of her mind and heart.

She wondered where Thad and Abby were at that moment, their lives, their world shattered. She touched her bruised throat, tried to feel anger. Anger was easier than pain, than pity. She thought of Chance firing the shot into the air. Chance, who'd stayed at the hospital all night long, but who'd never stopped at the house. Anger was easier than pain.

A car turned into the drive and for a moment her whole body tensed. Then she sagged. It was not the red truck. Father Jake crawled out of his ancient Toyota and plodded wearily to the steps.

"Jervey." The seraphic face was drawn with exhaustion. "I was afraid you'd gone to bed." He put his hands on her shoulders, examined her under the veranda light. "I would have come sooner, but I was with Thad and Abby all day."

"I'm glad. Would you like to come in?"

"No, dear. It's late. You seem all right."

"Yes." Abruptly her eyes filled with tears. "No! No, I'm

not. I don't understand, Father Jake. I just can't understand."

"I know. Believe me, I know."

"Thad—I've known him since I was a teenager. He was such a good person. People depended on him, went to him for help. He cared. I know he cared."

"You're right, he did. In the beginning. Oh Jervey, it's hard to understand. He had a gift with people, a God-given gift, but, somewhere in his life, he forgot that it was a gift. Like Lucifer, he was a bright star in the firmament, an instrument of grace. Then, at some crucial point, he assumed that he was the grace, the power. He fell."

"And Abby?"

"I think Abby's sin was against the First Commandment. Thad became her God."

Jervey couldn't hold back the tears running down her cheeks. "I can't handle it, Father Jake."

"Yes you can. All of us must."

"How?" It was a cry.

"By asking for the grace to forgive."

He put his arms around her and kissed her wounded head, then turned and, like a very old man, walked to his car.

When Jervey went back in the house, the first thing she noticed was Stanley's beribboned box of candy, still lying on the hall table. She hoped to heaven he hadn't seen it, still sitting there, still unopened.

Tired as she was, she couldn't sleep. Oddly, her thoughts were not of Thad and Abby, the horror, the pain. She found herself thinking of Keith Lynch, the violent end of his young life, the terrible waste. She felt as if she'd known him, the charming, gifted actor, the appealing man Elissa had fallen in love with, the mysterious loner. Ten years ago no friend or kin had been expecting him to arrive from Oldport. No inquiries were made. She wondered if he'd been an orphan or maybe estranged from parents who still hoped he'd one day

206

walk through the door. So far, no one had mourned his death. Lying in bed, looking through the window at the almost-leafless tree, thinly glazed with moonlight, she grieved at the passing of a man she'd never known.

Nineteen

· · · · ·

She had no nightmares. She dreamed that she was a child again, dancing on the veranda in a ballet costume Hap had made for her fifth birthday.

She didn't lie in bed after she'd wakened. By the time Roberta appeared in her doorway, she had closed her suitcase, checked bureau and closet to make sure she'd not forgotten anything.

"Emma's all packed," announced Roberta. "I got a suitcase from the attic to hold the extras she's acquired. What about breakfast?"

"I'm not hungry, Ma."

"I called Chance last night before I went to bed, told him the show would go on."

"Good."

"I don't see why you won't let Milo or me drive you to the Charleston airport. Those rental cars from Sam Griffin's look pretty seedy."

"Ma, I hate farewells at airports. You know that."

"We could just drop you there."

"No."

"Wretched child."

"Manipulating Mama."

Roberta walked across the room and sat on the window seat. "I talked to El Sparkman this morning. Thad finally made a complete confession. El said it was really weird, like a report at an annual meeting. I keep thinking how stunned the two of them must have been to see that mummy case onstage. All those years of not being sure, then gradually beginning to feel safe, home free." She glanced at Jervey. "You don't want to talk about it, do you?"

"No, Ma."

"I understand. Jervey, listen, you're not only in mourning for Thad and Abby, the terrible betrayal, you're grieving for the loss of something as important as breath, the loss of trust. Don't let it go on too long. Let yourself heal. Self-trust, intuition—it's a bleak life without them, an eternal groping in the dark. Somewhere down the line you've got to begin again to trust your own heart."

Milo had prepared a splendid farewell meal, tournedos of beef Héloise, small roasted potatoes, artichokes vinaigrette, and apple flan. Emma, subdued, ate with polite determination. She stopped every few minutes to inspect her new bracelet, delicate gold links with a beautifully wrought charm, clasped hands, a gift from Roberta and Milo.

"You know, I still can't get over Evelyn Carroll," said Roberta. "Of course, I had a feeling she might be good, but only because, well, after what happened, we were due some small miracle."

Milo watched Emma carefully finishing her flan. "I've noticed that shy, insecure people often make good actors. They need an alternate life, I guess."

"What's an alternate life?" asked Emma.

"An escape. The chance to be a different person for a little while."

Emma pondered on this. "Is that why Chance is so good?"

"No." Milo took a sip of wine. "Chance isn't shy or insecure. I think he's good because he sets up no barriers. He's willing to take risks."

Jervey rose. "Emma, I think we'd better get going."

Roberta drove Jervey to Sam Griffin's Car Rentals, a shabby building and parking lot down near the waterfront. Sam, a small, spidery man, looked up at Jervey with curiosity and sympathy. "You been through a lot. Now I'll have a man at the Charleston airport right at your gate to pick up the car, help with your bags. He's a big bald fellow. You can't miss him." He stared at the bandage on Jervey's forehead. "I just can't believe what happened to you. I'll bet those bigwigs at Accrolux are in a tizzy. This thing's really rocked the town."

Milo had brought the suitcases to the veranda by the time they got back to the house. In silence they packed the small car. Twice Emma had to run into the house, first to get her bird guide and then her notebook. Roberta produced a package of sandwiches and cookies. "Airline food can be the pits."

Their good-byes had a formal, almost theatrical cheerfulness with promises to call and write, assurances that Christmas would arrive before they knew it, break-a-leg wishes for the play. Emma, back straight, head erect, shook hands with Roberta and Milo and hurried to the car.

"Emma!" called Roberta suddenly.

Emma turned, looked toward the veranda.

"I have this friend," said Roberta. She walked to the bottom step, smiled. "I have this friend."

With a little half sob, all formality gone, Emma ran to Roberta's arms. Jervey stared at the steering wheel, waited for Emma to climb in beside her.

"Wait!" yelled Milo. He ran into the house and returned

210

at once, holding Stanley's beribboned box of candy. He hurried to the car, opened the back door, and threw it on the seat. "Treats for the trip," he said.

They headed north, driving through the town, past the extensive Accrolux development, and finally reached the old highway. On either side stretched the marshland, its long grass gilded in the last rays of the sun. Jervey thought of the barrier islands and the sea on her right and, to the left, the wide savannas and the pine forests. She thought of all she'd seen that day in the canoe, the sense of life-forms all around her, the sense of life itself.

"Look!" Emma was pressed to the window, watching a long-legged white bird rise from the marsh grass.

"A heron?"

"No," corrected Emma. She rolled down her window. "An egret. You can tell by its bill."

Emma hung out the window in a fever of observation. During the next hour she identified a marbled godwit, an oystercatcher, and a turnstone, pausing now and then to check her bird guide and notebook.

But Emma finally turned to her. She tried to speak casually. "How much farther is it?"

"Not far."

Emma sank back on the seat, put the bird guide and notebook in her worn knapsack.

Jervey longed to distract her, console her, promise her that they would do exciting things when they got back to New York. But the words wouldn't come. She felt numb. Finally, pulling herself together, she was able to speak with a semblance of brightness. "Emma, let's take a look at Stanley's box of candy. Maybe it's a bunch of surprises, really good stuff."

"I don't much like boxes of candy," said Emma. "Someone's always holding out a box of chocolates and telling me to take one and, when I take one, it's always got jelly inside."

"Maybe you'll get lucky. I know what, we'll each keep taking one until we get what we want. We'll throw all the jellies out the window."

Emma giggled. Moving onto her knees, she reached back and, after a few attempts, grabbed the box. Sitting again, she undid the blue ribbons.

"It sure looks fancy, Jervey."

"No piker, Stanley."

For several seconds, Emma didn't speak.

"What's the matter? Can you spot the jellies?"

"There aren't any jellies. There's no candy."

"What?" With a sinking feeling Jervey envisioned more jewelry.

"No candy at all. Just string. A ball of string and an envelope with your name on it."

"String?"

"And under the string some leaves, red and yellow."

Jervey slowed the car. "String?"

"It's not from Stanley, is it?"

"No." Jervey pulled over to the side of the road, turned off the engine. As she took the envelope, Emma, again at the window, cried out, "There's a hawk! I'm sure it's a hawk."

The message was handwritten on plain white paper. It was not long and she read it twice. She picked up the ball of string, clean new string, tightly wound, then put the note and the string back in the box. She started the car, turned on the empty highway, and headed back south. Emma wheeled to look at her, speechless for once.

"Don't ask," said Jervey.

They didn't talk. Jervey was aware that every few minutes, Emma, her cheeks bright pink, would turn and stare at her. It was Emma who, filled with sudden hope, became too excited for silence. She started to sing. She sang old songs from *The Sound of Music*. She sang new songs that Jervey didn't know. Finally she launched into "Amazing Grace" and Jervey sang with her.

They sailed past the stretching marshes, past pine forests. Finally they left behind the Accrolux plant, the outskirts of town. The town itself seemed to swim in a soft rose light. When they at last reached the house, Jervey saw that both Roberta's and Milo's cars were there. As soon as they drew up near the veranda steps, Emma was out of the car, starting to run.

"Tell Ma I'll phone," called Jervey. She watched Emma dash up the steps and head for the front door. Before Emma's loud knock could be answered, Jervey was again starting down the street.

She knew the way. As she drove along the two-lane highway, she recognized an abandoned motel, a small gas station, peeling signs for Major Bob's chewing tobacco and Dixie Moon homemade sausage. There were fewer and fewer cinderblock houses, an occasional cypress hut. Long shafts of fading light slanted through the trees on either side.

It wasn't until she turned in to the narrow dirt road that she allowed herself to think. In a great rush she was enveloped by thoughts, by the voice of reason, the voice of doubt. She stopped the car, sat trembling.

All the disillusion, disappointments of her young life rose up to assail her, defeat her. She thought of her flawed perceptions of people, Jason, Abby, Thad. She thought of the cost.

She took the letter from the box, opened it. She thought of it lying on the hall table since Friday night, this letter that could mean nothing or everything.

Twice you asked why I agreed to be in the play. I guess I wasn't ready to answer. When I saw you for the first time that day in church, I didn't hear Father Jake's prayers or the hymns or what I was saying. I kept thinking of when I was a kid and

213

my father took me up near Charleston to see something extraordinary. Just outside town, someone had spotted a Bachman's warbler, a bird that was thought to be extinct. Birders came from all over to see it, one man from California. While I was looking through Dad's binoculars at this little bird on a pine branch, he told me I was having a once-in-a-lifetime experience and to remember it always. He told me I must train my eye to spot the treasures. I did.

She stared at the letter, the ball of string. Not "no strings" but a new, clean, tightly wound ball of string. She turned on the ignition, started again through the dusk down the dirt road.

She saw lights in the cottage. The red truck was parked near the dock. She drew up beside it, got out, waited. She watched the door of the cottage open, watched him come out, discover her standing there. She saw his look of amazement turn to something she could only identify as joy. She filled her eyes with him as he came toward her, moving with his own singular grace. It was the grace of a man who, long ago, might have tracked with Indians, the grace of a man who, somewhere in the future, could teach a child to taste the wind.